# *Taming* ALEXANDER

# Taming ALEXANDER

Leo Sparx

*Taming Alexander*

4 Horsemen Publications, Inc.
1497 Main St. Suite 169
Dunedin, FL 34698
4horsemenpublications.com
*info@4horsemenpublications.com*

Cover & Typesetting by Battle Goddess Productions
Editor Tilda M. Cooke



*Ebook ISBN: 978-1-64450-139-9*

*Paperback ISBN: 978-1-64450-140-5*

# Dedication

Fur Bryan
No otter boys combear!

## Queer Zoology

Otter (n): *a man who is leaner than a cub or bear but still covered in fur*

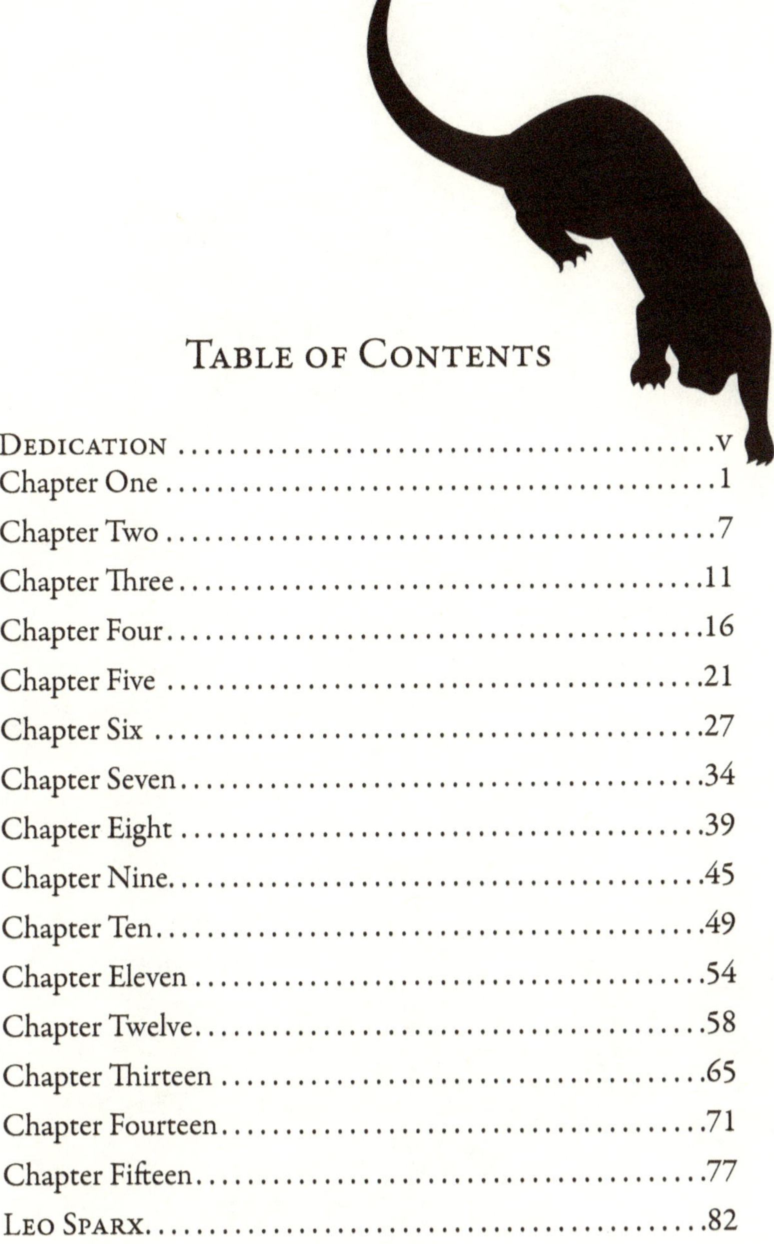

# Table of Contents

# Chapter One

Over a year ago, on the night I'd left Roderick in the rain, I didn't know where I was going. I only knew that if I was going to survive on my own, I needed to work. The boat launch became my new home. Near the brackish water, the boat launch was in a park where men would sit in their cars and wait for each other. Where they'd cruise from the safety of their silver four-door sedans or baby-blue SUVs until they saw someone they liked and ventured into the brush.

I'd tried the bathhouse before that, loitering near the exterior of a place that marketed itself as a men-only gym, but didn't have any workout equipment inside. The pretense of waiting for my workout buddy in hopes a customer would invite me in to share his rented room was exhausting, but it was the only way inside without paying my own admission. Even getting a locker for a few hours was out of my price-point as an initial investment to make a sale.

Pacing circles at the boat launch park and weaving through the used condoms in the sand near where the mangroves met with the bay water had a much lower overhead. I could spiral from there to the parking lot half a dozen times pretending I'd just arrived before a Daddy would notice and follow me through the long green and brown shoots and stems. Once we found an open spot, I'd ask him if he was feeling *generous* with doe-like eyes and a smile before I got to my knees in the wet sediment or bent over a pile of salty driftwood.

He had to know the code first. That being *generous* meant he was willing to pay for quality head or sex from a professional. But once the formalities were out of the way—regardless of how the low tax of the park often matched the general look of the clientele—it was typically worth the constant charade to finally score a paying customer.

Darius told me later, after I'd been in his house for a few months, that his approaching me at the boat launch hadn't been entirely selfless. Apparently, multiple men had complained about me lifting their wallets while they had their pants on the ground and word traveled fast. He wasn't angry when he pulled me aside that summer evening in the park, but he was direct in letting me know I was giving the boys doing legitimate sex work in town a bad name and cutting into his business. I was lucky to encounter him before anyone else who wanted to point out my mistake. Instead of creating an enemy, Darius offered me a room and a job. He gave me a place to stay and a safe space to turn tricks.

As I got to know my new roommates, Brent and Marco—the bleach-blonde brothers from the north—and Sonny—the kid with the long wavy hair who only stayed awake long enough to take dick and paper money—I realized we had more in common than we didn't. We all had different stories for how we ended up in the house Darius had somehow acquired. Even if the structure was falling apart and so filthy it could never be truly clean, it was more than most of us had ever had as a shelter once we'd become adults.

The stark contrast of my present surroundings in The House of Otter from my previous dwellings didn't escape me, even if the pleasantries from Usher seemed to be dwindling more with each passing day. When I'd received his most recent note, it was difficult to determine if he was angry with me:

> *White briefs.*
> *Downstairs.*
> *Now.*

If this had been just a few afternoons before, and especially after using the secret passage without explicit permission, I would have been filled with anxiety that this sudden request would mean my dismissal from the house, but after the experience with the three of us together—bound to Roderick and taking Usher's spit inside of me—I felt more secure. Even if the notion was a coping mechanism on my part, it had all been so ceremonial. Something about the encounter made things seem more official, as if part of a ritual had been completed.

Usher didn't have many words this evening. Upon my arrival in the room, he kept his back toward me, simply instructing that I sit on a black metal block and remove the briefs I had just been told to put on. *Make up your mind*, I thought, but didn't speak. My balls and bare ass were frosty upon the block as I watched him gather toys and whips on a table, then wheel the giant wooden X, the one he had called a Saint Andrew's Cross, into the center of the room.

I was seated to the side of the structure in a section of the room which gave me an unobstructed view of his preparation, and I held my breath as I watched him give each whip a snap against the table, choosing the perfect weapon. There didn't seem to be a way to physically prepare for the pain, but I exhaled and hugged my knees to my chest trying to convince myself that whatever he was about to inflict upon my skin would only be temporary. I let myself hope there was always a chance I could find his eyes and convince him to handle me with more care.

Even if part of me was still confused by the ebb and flow of our intimacy—not to mention the physical anger he consistently showed toward Roderick, and the way he was keeping us separated from each other—my craving for his cock and touch seemed to outweigh my anger and confusion anytime I was in his presence.

When Usher seemed pleased with his selections, he walked toward me and said, "Don't move, boy."

I nodded before he ran his sprawling palm through my hair, letting his fingers wrap around to give a light tug while he used his other hand to push my legs back into a position to leave me exposed. The motions made me close my eyes and bite my lip. I waited, trying to anticipate his next move, the punishment I hadn't yet received for venturing into the woods and attempting to contact Darius.

When I'd used the keys to open the wardrobe which led to the passage, I didn't know who had provided them. It wasn't until I found the phone and colored shells strategically placed in the trees that I knew Roderick had been the one orchestrating my first peek at an alternative exit from the manor. There was an endless list of actions Usher could decide were violations at any time, even if I hadn't known the acts were against the rules while committing them.

The keeper of the house I'd chosen seemed to adhere to a policy I'd first discovered while handcuffed in the back of a police car. When three cops surrounded me with their dicks out at the boat ramp, and I'd been tasked to give the blowbang of my life in exchange for my freedom. I thought about the imaginary itemized missteps I'd made since accepting my place as his boy: enjoying Roderick's body, using the hidden passage without permission, and leading Darius to the house. As if Usher had said them himself, the cop's words from the experience before my life here echoed in my mind: "Ignorance of the law is not an excuse."

Usher released my hair, and for a few seconds, I lingered in the expectation of a slap or a tail snapping at my nakedness, but instead, when I opened my eyes again, he was gone. The brighter lights in the room were off, and the corner I was in had turned mostly to darkness. He had closed the door behind him, and the ominous low tones I hadn't realized were missing before were suddenly cued-up and playing.

It seemed colder now. The white briefs I had worn were still balled up on the cement near my feet. I was high enough that my soles didn't touch the ground, and as I waited, I let my heels tap rhythmically against the hollow block with nervous tension. So many of the sexual games Usher orchestrated seemed to be about the waiting, demonstrating submission through patience. It reminded me of clients other boys had told me about who liked to be kept in confinement more than engage in a physical encounter. I'd always wondered what those men thought about in their cages, if they could reach a state of meditative euphoria from simply being left alone. Solitude I could manage, and previous to this life, often needed. But I was still uncertain whether I found the idea of being a kept object as arousing as being financially secure.

A bang came from outside, then another. I stopped swinging my heels as the metal of the chamber door rattled in response to the exterior noise. Following the series of sounds and joining in the haunting chorus of spooky Halloween tones was a constant screaming of indistinguishable words. They were the peaks and valleys of a voice I'd gotten very familiar with over the last year, one that had woken me for late lunches and early dinners of mostly juice concentrate, someone who had given me shelter when I was in desperate need.

Now here he was being dragged through the door with Usher's firm grip around his socks at the ankle, pulled the same way I had in what I still tried to convince myself had been a dream. Usher was busy forcing Darius's body, which I could see now was clothed in something tight and black, through the door, but he took just a moment to acknowledge me in the corner. Seeing how I observed the scene, he pierced me with his eyes in a way that made his last words reverberate through me, "Don't move, boy."

# Chapter Two

I wanted to trust Usher, to assume that he had my happiness in mind no matter what, but watching him hoist Darius toward the giant X made me want to leap toward them both. Instead, I stayed paralyzed while Usher secured each of Darius's feet and hands away from each other. He had forced Darius's shirt inside his mouth as a gag. From where I sat, I could see everything, including Usher's smirk as he ran his fingers through the furry body hair that seemed longer and thicker than I remembered it being on my former roommate's body. His typically smooth face was now covered in a longer stubble that Usher took the time to vigorously stroke. Darius didn't have a view of me and my inaction, but his stifled screams made me shiver.

Thinking back to the night I'd sat outside the French doors waiting for Roderick inside this house, my mind filled in some blanks I hadn't let myself think about before. Roderick had known exactly what he was doing, leading me to Usher's home and within his grasp, letting me believe I was somehow safe outside while he probably helped Usher with the elaborate setup in this very room. I'd worried about him then, concerned that someone inside the house was harming him and I may need to come to his rescue. In reality, he was the one who could have chosen to save me before I officially began the process of becoming one of Usher's toys. Instead, he'd remained quiet while he heard my screams and pleading for release. Roderick had sat naked in this spot and watched Usher administer the first steps. He'd known the whole time we dressed together in his fake apartment that I was going to cum on his favorite pair of black pants.

I'd seen Darius's cock and balls so many times they were nearly committed to my memory. He'd always been attractive to me in a traditional sort of way, like how I would appreciate a tree with perfect branches or a beautiful scent. That's not to say we haven't fucked before. Shortly after I moved into the house, we'd absolutely fooled around. Neither one of us hinted at our interest in each other, but I was thankful for his hospitality, and as I had learned to do in life, demonstrated my gratitude in a physical manner.

It wasn't that it wasn't good or enjoyable for us both, but as much as we flirted after that night, we never messed around again. Our relationship became brotherly. Darius was my family and meant more to me as a mature sibling I could rely on for advice and understanding than a convenient fuck buddy. He'd continuously defended me to the other boys in the house when I was short on rent, and now he was further demonstrating his reliability by showing up here. I hadn't sent for him nor asked him to come, but I had made contact with him. I'd put him in a position to find out where I was and worry about saving me. Still, I was uncertain if that was the reason he showed up at the manor looking for a door or if his invitation had come from Usher himself.

Even considering my familiarity with the perfection of Darius's setup, seeing his thick cock released through the zipper of the dark pants he wore by Usher's large hand made my breath quake. From where I sat motionless, I couldn't take my eyes off of either of them. As Usher began stroking Darius's firmness, I wasn't able to hide that between my spread legs over the corner of the block, my own cock rose and dripped precum down my shaft. I tried not to draw attention, not to touch myself or look at how quickly I was growing. There was no way to hide my reaction, no throw pillows or blankets. The minimalist nature of Usher's favorite room left little to the imagination, and my nakedness only added to the aesthetic's lack of nuance.

Usher stroked Darius with a tight lubricated fist, occasionally taunting him with the whips on the table but never making contact with his skin. With his hand pushing the saliva-covered shirt deeper into Darius's mouth, Usher made eye contact with me, then looked immediately at my hard cock. I hadn't noticed when I'd been in Darius's place on the giant X whether or not Usher had been looking off to the side or behind where I was fastened in place, but if Roderick had been there the whole time observing the domination, it had been for the same reason I was here now. This was another test.

Usher's face displayed disappointment with my erectness, complete betrayal at the moistness building up below my foreskin and pushing its way out to trickle down between my hairy thighs and to the metal block. But he raised his eyebrows—not just with permission, but insistence—a non-verbal command to touch and stroke myself. My first instinct was to resist, and still, I worried his approval was yet another layer of his game, the tests he so often administered with the hope I would fail. He didn't need a reason to punish me, but he seemed to enjoy making me feel as if I'd forced his hand. In certain ways, I suppose I did as well, since defying him often meant more of his attention.

Ignoring the pulsing, which continued as I heard Darius approaching climax, was unbearable. I knew his sounds from the time I'd swallowed him, but also the countless encounters he'd had inside our house with customers. From his expression, I couldn't tell if he was aroused in spite of himself or if he truly wanted Usher to force out and claim his cum. His eyes widened, and his breath quickened in rhythm with my own. I wanted us to shoot at the same time, but it wasn't just him turning me on. It was the domination; it was Usher and his commanding presence. I wasn't jealous about him touching other boys the way I assumed I would be when he'd told me about his various estates. Observing the way he worked, the commitment to allowing a new boy to have a full experience, only made me want him more.

Pumping at my cock now with the tips of my fingers first and then my whole closed fist, I knew it wasn't going to take much for me to expel my load. Usher was staring into Darius's eyes, the way he had when I'd been the new boy restrained and at his mercy. He was commanding him to cum, and Darius complied as more spit dripped from the sides of the drenched fabric gag. While his last spurt ran down the open fly of his pants, Usher's eyes moved to mine with a similar demand, and I shot hard, trying my best not to make a sound. I was compliant in his game. Not only had I watched the entire thing, I'd enjoyed it.

Staring at the cement floor, I wondered who was tasked with cleaning up the mess every time it was covered in cum. Darius seemed to be motionless now, his body relaxed and his head resting on his chest. After taking a small taste from his finger, Usher wiped the cum and lube from his hands then removed the restraints from Darius's wrists and ankles. He cleaned him up, fastened his pants, hoisted Darius's full weight onto his shoulder, and carried him in my direction. Before exiting through the metal door, Usher looked at my soft cock and the release I'd left on the forest of hair covering my pubic bone. He shook his head with disapproval before disappearing through the door toward the hallway. I'd done exactly as he'd commanded, and yet, I had still somehow failed his test.

# Chapter Three

Several minutes elapsed before I could hear Usher's heavy footsteps approaching the entrance again. If the music had stopped, I would have assumed it was time for me to return to my room, but it still chimed with mysterious bells and electronic rhythms. I hadn't moved at all in the short amount of time he was gone, even to wipe myself off, and I was thankful to learn I had finally made a correct decision when he saw me still in place and said, "Good boy. I'm not done with you yet."

It felt good to hear kind words, even if I could sense punishment looming in the air. He'd hardly used the whips laid out at all, and I worried that every tool he had chosen was intended especially for me.

My guess was that he'd returned Darius to the porch in the courtyard with the stone men, that the French doors were again bolted shut, and he'd be leaving him out there until Darius came directly to him—as I had. It was speculation on my part, but there did seem to be a pattern, some sort of method to the ritual our keeper coordinated for each of us.

"You shouldn't have cum," Usher said, tracing his hand over one of the longer paddles he had on the table. "This is all going to hurt a lot more now." His back was to me as he analyzed the tools and toys he'd collected.

Often he stayed in his fancy clothes: a suit, sometimes a tie, like today. He hadn't even removed his navy jacket while he'd played with Darius. But now he did and left it hanging over one arm of the Saint Andrew's Cross. He loosened his slim matching tie and unbuttoned the top button of his crisp white shirt. His formal attire so often felt like an intentional division between us, a wealthy man in contrast to my lower-class status, his hidden body to my near constant nudity. From my perspective, the fitted suit was the sigil of man who took his business seriously, but even more so, it was a symbol of his power over me.

Perhaps it was the relaxation that came with ejaculation, but before I could overthink what I was saying, the question slipped from my lips. "What did I do?"

Usher cracked the side of his mouth in a half-smile while he removed the silver cufflinks from his shirt. "I had hoped you would be different, boy," he said, rolling up his sleeves. "But just like your friend, you've disappointed me. I offer you gifts and you use them to show me you cannot be trusted."

He turned his eyes to the spot where I'd rolled around with Roderick while he watched just a few nights before. It felt like so much time had passed between then and now, from the last evening I'd touched Roderick or had even seen him physically. I wondered what it had been like for him, to observe from the corner I was seated in now, while I'd been the one secured to the wooden structure. With the straps around my wrists and legs while Usher's hand tugged at my cock, I imagined he must have seen everything. From the moment Roderick had left me alone in the dark courtyard until I'd been dragged back unconscious and returned to the cold stone, I could only assume he'd witnessed it all as I had tonight with Darius.

So much of my interpretation of what Usher said relied on what he didn't say between his carefully chosen words, but one recently vocalized selection stuck out to me: *disappointed.* If he was comparing me to Roderick then I had replicated something he'd done in the same position. Recalling the way Usher had punished him immediately after that first initiation, I wanted to understand how I had just potentially earned the same treatment for myself.

"Perhaps this new boy will make up for your short-comings." Usher traced his fingertips over the sweat Darius had left behind on the wood. Rolling the wetness between his fingers and thumb, he brought the moisture to his mouth, dragged the salty liquid across his bottom lip, and smiled. While his tongue curled around his lips to taste the residue, my blood ran scalding hot then immediately ice cold. I should have been happy Darius would be in the house with me soon, but I sensed that Usher wasn't bringing him in for me to have a companion; he was using him to challenge me further.

"Why him?" I asked and inhaled deeply, my anger forcing itself past my better judgement to question a man within reach of a full selection of disciplinary objects. Usher caressed the handle of a whip wrapped in dark ribbons of coarse black material before raising his eyes to mine.

"Afraid of temptation?" He curled his fist around something but kept it behind his back and out of my view. The choice had been made.

"Temptation?" I wasn't certain what he was talking about, but as a reply to my confusion, he nodded to the sticky droplets drying on my stomach and his floor. The metal block still housed small translucent domes sitting between my bare legs and soft cock. As he pointed toward them it became more clear: he thought I wanted to fuck Daruis. That had been the test I'd failed. He wanted to know if he could trust me around his newest addition to the mansion. And like Roderick must have done when he'd been my ambassador to the lifestyle within the manor, I'd gotten hard from the display of Usher asserting his power over a boy.

I didn't have the words to explain right away, to tell Usher that as sexy as Darius was, he hadn't been the one I was looking at while I came. Usher had commanded my nakedness and vulnerability, he'd provided an atmosphere of sexual dominance. Observing him commanding a load from Darius's body as he had from me the first time I'd felt his grasp around my cock—that was what had brought me to such a state of arousal, and it was only his insistence that led me to believe I should shoot. It had been for him.

As much as I'd been thinking about Roderick since I'd felt his lips on mine, I couldn't deny the craving I still had for Usher's body. At times, it was even stronger than my need for his approval. But I didn't know how to tell him. While I'd watched him demonstrating his power, it was him I wanted, to be back in that place and restrained with my cock exposed for Usher's enjoyment, responding to his demands. If not being aroused by his interaction with Darius had been the test, I hadn't failed exactly. Not in the way he was insinuating.

But with Usher approaching where I sat with the mysterious whip concealed behind his back, I couldn't plead my case before I felt several hard stings across my chest. Now revealed, the weapon he'd decided upon had more tails than I'd seen before and twisted knots at the end. My skin burned as he pushed his free hand into my open mouth to force me on my back. He tasted like salt and coins. It was Darius's sweat mixed with the metal surfaces of the red room Usher had been arranging when I'd initially arrived for the evening's event.

My back now flat on the coldness of the block, Usher grabbed both my ankles and took the knotted tails to my ass and thighs. I screamed out from the slashing pain while I used my hands on either side of the surface to steady myself in place, making an active effort not to resist. Usher had somehow managed to palm both my feet together and knowing he could do so with one hand made me bite my lower lip, fighting a smile. Something felt right about being at his mercy again. Being restrained while he paused for just a moment from the lashings to poke the base of the whip at my balls and soft cock, felt even better.

# Chapter Four

"You're going to regret not leaving any loads in there for me, boy," Usher said, using the cylinder of the handle to give the thin hairy skin hanging between my legs a few lights taps. I struggled to keep in place and attempted to wiggle away from the sensation. He released his hold and allowed me to lay on my side for only a moment to breathe before pulling my legs out straight to force me to my stomach.

With my ass in the air, I heard the object he'd been using to beat me hit the cement somewhere near my drying cum and underwear. He pulled me by my waist with a quick motion to bring me to my hands and knees, then pushed my face toward the block until my cheek was flush with the metal, letting my ass spread open enough to expose my hole. At first I worried he would retreat to the table for a toy or something else to force inside me, but instead, I felt the familiar fabric of his suit on the back of my thighs. With his pants brushing against the areas he had hit with the tails, my skin felt raw and singed.

The only pleasure came when I felt the hardness of him behind the fly of his pants pushing against me. Despite the delicate state of my backside, I thrust back and wiggled my ass over his firmness, hoping my body would reassure him he was desired. A reward came swiftly as his belt buckle clinked against itself. I could feel the warmth of his cock pulsing against my hole and within seconds even warmer spit from his mouth dropping to the tightness.

"It's going to hurt, boy," he said, using his cockhead to spiral the saliva around my opening. I was mentally aroused from feeling him so close to the precipice of fucking me, but wasn't getting hard. It hadn't been enough time since I'd spilled my load to be ready to offer another. Usher was right. Having him fuck me was going to be painful, but any opportunity I had to feel him inside was an opportunity I was going to take.

"Tell me, boy." I could feel his head forcing its way inside already, just teasing and pulling back out, making the pucker between my furry cheeks open and close around his girth. The silkiness of his precum slowly dripped beyond the threshold of my hole, and I imagined it going deeper. I wanted it to slide inside me while I waited for his cock and cum to follow. Curving my hands around the top of the hard surface in preparation, I nodded in response to his request.

"No. Say it, boy," he commanded. I hadn't noticed before that water had pooled in my eyes from the beating, but now the tears ran salty and warm to the block along with perspiration from my chest, armpits, and hair.

"Please fuck me!" I yelled out. "I need you to feel you!" With no further teasing or hesitation, he pushed his hips forward and plunged the entire length of himself past the entrance of my ass. I gasped with a rush of pain and stiffened my grip on the side of the block. He grabbed me by the hips and propelled his cock in a solid rhythm, never missing a chance to feed me every inch of himself after pulling out halfway.

There was something different about being fucked after I'd gotten off. It wasn't the first time, but it was the only time I'd known the discomfort was inevitable and had asked for it directly. Not experiencing the physical act for my own enjoyment as much as just being accessed for someone else's wasn't a new sensation, but having Usher use me as a hole for his satisfaction felt like a victory. My own precum drizzled from my foreskin again at the realization, adding to the collection of liquids under my body.

"Know that you won't have any of them without my permission, boy," he said, grabbing my hair from behind and making me crane my neck upward.

"I only want you!" Again the words escaped before I processed their full meaning, but in that moment, it didn't feel like I was lying. It wasn't my intention to give him lip-service just to earn his cum, but with immediacy, a familiar moan resonated between the surfaces of the room and his release was within me.

Unlike the previous times he'd defied his own rules, Usher didn't take the opportunity to leave directly after he came. Instead, he stayed buried in my depths and along with the temperature I'd become accustomed to, his cock remained where he had finished. I could feel him growing softer as we both basked in the warmth, but his hand moved from the back of my hair to my lower back, where his fingers caressed my skin, tracing lines and words I couldn't understand. My fur bristled under the unanticipated gentle touch, and it took all of me to stay in place, to not turn around and sneak a kiss somewhere above his beard but below his dark mustache.

I thought about his lips but knew any sudden movement would make him slip out of me. I intended to savor the uncharacteristic gesture as long as possible. If I did turn to face him and dared put my mouth on his, the whip and collection of unused paddles were still within his reach. Pushing his boundaries had worked before to gain some form of his affection, but our encounters were so few and far between that when I gained the opportunity to interact with him, I didn't want to risk tainting it.

A satisfied moan escaped me, something animalistic and unplanned. I ached for more of him, and I wondered if he knew. Almost in response from behind me, Usher grunted with a tone I could only recognize as guilt and immediately withdrew himself from me.

"You've ruined me, boy," he said, refastening his belt. My ass and chest both burned from the fury he had inflicted with the tails upon my skin. I didn't want to sit on my tender thighs to turn toward him, but I needed to see his face. Balancing on my palms, I spun slowly until I could rest on my knees. My cock was still dripping, and with my ass now hovering over my ankles, my hole was so open Usher's cum leaked out to add to the mess I'd left on the block.

He looked down at my cock, still not fully erect but obviously affected, and smirked. I couldn't believe he was still in the room with me at all, but I searched for the right words to ask him what had made him stay. My mind cycled through the combination of letters I could use to ask him what he meant when he said I had *ruined* him, but my body kept the blood it needed for deep thoughts in my pulsing cock. Nothing in my brain was processing correctly. I felt dizzy and knew I was only seconds away from losing his attention.

Before my better judgement could kick in, my mouth put it simply. "How did I ruin you?" It wasn't my most articulate turn of phrase, but with my body in such a state, I was impressed that some part of me had managed to form words at all.

Usher gathered his cufflinks and jacket. As he reassembled his more familiar polished facade, he sighed. "You'll find a phone in your room when you return, boy. Not the one you and your friend have been using to deceive me. When you receive my messages, do only as you're told."

He was by the door when he reached into his pocket, and the music stopped. The magic trick revealed in some capacity that as I had imagined, Usher did control the tones from some remote device on his person. That explained how the lights and atmosphere timed so well to any action performed inside the manor. In a certain way, I was disappointed to see behind the curtain, as if he'd decided I was no longer worth the illusion, smoke, and mirrors, that I didn't deserve his show.

"Your other friend will be among us shortly I'm sure. Make him comfortable, and understand boy, I have moved the world for you. Do not disappoint me." His words were stern as the door to the red room slid open into the hallway. Before he disappeared into the grandness of the house, he turned toward me one last time.

"This is not how we do things here. Be assured, when I return, this will not happen again." The overhead lights lit the room at full-power, bringing my attention to the ceiling. The brightness revealed more of the room than I had ever seen before, and it felt like being in an empty theme park directly after sunrise. I hadn't seen him push any new buttons or reach into his pocket to turn the lights on. When I looked back to the doorway, he was gone.

I smiled and let my wrecked body relax onto the semen-covered block. Perhaps he did still have magic left for me after all.

# Chapter Five

Cooking had never been among my talents. I can suck a dick like a downspout in a category five hurricane, but gathering ingredients and following a recipe? The text Usher had sent telling me it was time to make lunch may as well have been asking me to teach advanced calculus or translate Latin poetry. It was the chopping that seemed impossible from the start. I couldn't figure out the right knife in the kitchen I'd gained access to that would cut the vegetables well enough to throw in one of the hanging pots or pans. There were just too many options.

When the map I'd received over my new piece of technology led me to the library not far from my room, I wasn't expecting further instructions to lead me to a solid bookcase pressed against a wall. Below the map Usher had sent was the title of a book I'd never heard of before and had definitely never read. When I pulled the textured cover from the spot it sat sandwiched between other bound books, the bookcase slid to the side. After the incident with the credenza on my first real night with Usher and my discovery in my own room, seeing the stone passage was less surprising, but after following the tunnel and having it eventually open up into a giant industrial kitchen on the first floor and finding a skimpy apron with "boy" embroidered on it waiting, I had to admit there was no way to get used to the endless mystery of the house. Every day new secrets—whether strange, wonderful, or terrifying—seemed to reveal themselves.

Usher, of course, requested in a new text that I wear the apron—only the apron—while I cooked. This sounded sexy in theory, especially after spotting the cameras in every corner of the massive room and knowing he would be watching while I did my best imitation of a chef. In reality, once the blades were out to trim the tips from thick carrots and everything was heated to boiling temperatures or spitting oil, with the ties of the apron hanging from the knot and slipping into the crack of my ass, I felt more like a walking safety violation than the seductive star of *Cooking With Otters.* My assumption was the fantasy show, of course, was somehow being broadcast directly to Usher. If anyone else could see me mostly naked and on my tip toes trying to reach a large pot without it falling directly on my head, I wasn't certain.

What I did know for sure was Darius had made it inside the house. My initial hint that things had gone well after Usher left me alone in the red room was the first text on my new phone asking me what sort of food I thought Darius may enjoy. The truth was I had rarely seen him eat. I knew he preferred wintergreen-flavored condoms and had an affinity for a particular brand of cherry lubricant that dyed his white sheets pink at one point, but otherwise, extra money in the home I'd shared with the boys infrequently went toward groceries. Anything that didn't come from a value menu or gas station rotisserie was crunchy crumbs in an aluminum bag or some bright liquid in a paper carton. In our lives, hunger was rarely a culinary opportunity as much as an inconvenience.

Darius had told me before about the dishes his grandmother used to prepare for him before he moved away. Once when he was feeling nostalgic for home and had hit a particularly large payday with a client, he came home with brown paper bags full of non-processed ingredients. He laid out a rainbow of vegetables and cooked them among infused oils and fresh garlic. With the entire house of boys, he shared a piece of himself that we knew he missed terribly. He served what he told us was a stew with rice on paper plates. That night was the most at home I had ever felt with the boys, all sitting in our underwear on the dirty carpet because we didn't have a table, but smiling and moaning happily through every bite. The cooked spices lingered in the air and lasted for days until the tupperware containers packed with leftovers were scraped down to remnants, and we licked them clean with our fingers and tongues.

Those were the only items I could remember, that single recipe and meal he had shared with us. So it was what I texted back to Usher as a shopping list and what was now laid out in front of me on a stainless steel counter—deconstructed. The array of ingredients meant that Darius was still here and Usher intended to introduce him to the type of comfort and luxury he could expect under his care. They also meant that, like Roderick had been instructed to do for me, I was tasked with preparing meals for Darius...who, unfortunately, was about to be very disappointed with my poor interpretation of his grandmother's famous stew.

It was my fault he was here at all, and knowing what physical abuse he had already encountered at Usher's hands, I wanted to offer my best apology, even if he wouldn't know for sure it was from me.

I could open cans almost flawlessly, and as I shook the organic broth with both fists, I noticed the monitor for the first time. Whoever was typically in this kitchen had the ability to observe the various occupied rooms on a single screen mounted near the plates and bowls at eye-level. I recognized my room first, the huge empty bed and closed wardrobe. A few seconds later the screen flashed and the image was a rotating view of the purple bathtub. During my entire stay, the people in here had been able to see me in the bathroom. Fantastic.

The images continued to flip, mostly to empty and unfamiliar rooms with beds that appeared untouched. When I did finally see movement, it was Darius pacing in his quarters. Surprisingly, he didn't seem upset as much as confused while he circled around, trying to force open all the doors and windows. I knew eventually he would give up and settle in. He had endured quite a night and must have anticipated more were to come. Hopefully, the food would help.

More unoccupied rooms cycled until a single shot of a bed with a naked ass and leg hanging from the covers made me stop chopping. I knew that hairy ass; it was Roderick. His room wasn't as cute as mine but suited him. Knowing he was surrounded by his beloved floor poufs made me happy, but the slight movement of his furry round butt got me hard instantly.

I didn't often experience the urge to top. In the past, other boys had told me the size I'd been gifted from the universe was wasteful. But in that moment, as Roderick's fuzzy peach sat waiting, I couldn't stop myself from imagining coming into his room and putting my tongue between his cheeks while he slept, getting the tight space between both sides of his fullness wet with my spit so I could pull myself out and tease the head of my cock around the perimeter of his hole until it pushed inside. I would pull him, still sleepy, up with my arm around his chest to rest my body on his bare back, then plunge deep inside of him while he got firmer and let the friction of the bedsheets tease his shaft while he rocked back and forth to let me fill him completely.

Growing hard, I put the knife down. I was certain it had been the wrong one to choose because it was hurting my palm.

Licking where the pain from the handle seared my etched lifeline, I allowed myself to pull the apron up enough to bring the lubrication to where my hardness was pushing through the material of the objectifying costume. The aroma of boiling starches filled the air, and my fingers were slightly orange from the grip I'd held while peeling the carrots as I wrapped my hand around my growing thickness. Everything around me was steaming hot and melding into an unintentional vegetable-based lubricant while I pulled at my cock and waited for the monitor to revolve back to Roderick's room. I needed another glimpse of his juicy ass.

When the video returned, I was so lost in my own thoughts of flipping him over on the bed to stroke his cock while I fucked him, of kissing him while our furry chests touched, that I didn't notice the sweet potatoes boiling over with foam and covering the burners. I didn't sense the sizzle or the smoke while I pumped my cock harder and harder looking at Roderick's exposed thighs in his bed. He looked as if he were waiting for me—if I could just find where his room was, I could have his tongue and cock in my mouth again.

By then I was shooting out from under the raised apron, spurts hitting the glass window of the oven I'd been preheating. Alarms were going off, and I slipped in my own cum trying to silence them. I wiped everything down with rags frantically while oil splattered and threatened my naked parts. I knew the rags would end up being stiff at some point from the combination of substances they were absorbing and, with the alarms still screeching, I waved the damp cloth at the smoke. The moisture spread in viscous strings around the kitchen from the towels, and with my bare ass and spent cock still exposed, the sirens finally died down.

Looking into the monitor, which was finally displaying Roderick's room again, I could see he was awake. The alarms and kitchen sounds I'd never heard from my room on the second floor were loud enough to wake him. He could hear them from where he stayed. I wanted to find him, to tell him that I finally knew for sure I shared the love he felt for me. But I knew with Usher's rules about us interacting it would never happen again without him supervising, that I'd never again feel Roderick's lips on mine unless I was obeying an order.

I had to least know he was safe, that he wasn't confined to his room forever or only released to be dealt constant punishment. He turned on his side, and for a second I thought I saw his cock looking half-hard, as if we'd been sharing my fantasy. Then just before the image on the monitor faded back to the montage of empty areas, he looked directly into the camera, and smiled.

# Chapter Six

The phone Usher had left for me was still a little confusing, but useful when real-time messages and maps came through to direct me to Darius's room and explain the passage from the library would be the quickest way from the kitchen to his room. I was still recovering from racing around the kitchen post-orgasm when he sent:

*Don't cum again until I return.*
*Your loads belong to me.*

Then immediately after:

*And clean that mess.*

He was definitely gone and had seen me jerkoff while I burned the bottom of every pot and pan in his kitchen, but I wondered if he had been able to zoom in close enough to see what had got me hard. It was difficult to know his intended inflection, but I let myself believe his text was almost playful. Still, I worried if he'd known the source of my motivation had been Roderick, he would have traveled immediately back to the mansion just to discipline us both.

Usher's recent map led me from the library bookcase to a room a few doors from my own room to deliver the hot food. Even if we couldn't interact, it was nice knowing Darius was close by, but I couldn't help to wonder what area of the house Roderick was confined in.

Since he'd heard the alarms when I'd burned Darius's lunch, there was a chance he was adjacent to the kitchen in several directions. He could be near it on the first floor or directly above. I hadn't thought before about searching for a basement in the manor. Being below sea-level didn't typically allow for underground structures, but we were in the country now, not Beachside, so there was a chance luxury could equate to secrets lying below the ground floor, leaving me even more options of where Roderick could be hidden away.

I was still only wearing the apron, but it was dingy now with food stains and hints of rogue ejaculate. The flat strings continued slipping into my ass crack as I walked with the full tray, threatening to untie and fall off my body as I neared the door indicated by Usher's description. If I had my bearings, Darius's window probably faced a similar area of the exterior woods as mine did.

Other than the distance a destination seemed to be from the areas I was familiar with, it was difficult to know for sure where I was at any time. The winding design of the hallways in the house made it impossible to know for sure without an aerial view, but I'd observed some of the layout had a system based on the colors of the walls and the paintings decorating them.

Once I set the food down, I'd need to take a left at the sexy nautical man with his groin area covered by rolling waves as he stood in the surf, then a right at the locked door near the framed portrait of a man wearing a top hat and a light blue jockstrap with one leg up on a short stool. Unlike the first story which maintained a steady theme of dark burgundy with gold accents, the second floor was mostly deep green walls which framed the portraits and lined the path back to the open bookcase in the library.

As far as breadcrumb trails go, the paintings and statues definitely weren't difficult markers to look at or memorize for future enjoyment. Every piece of art Usher had included in the house was sensual. Even the ones where a guy was bound or gagged, sometimes with a look of fear, still presented an artistic vision which couldn't be denied.

If he'd had these works commissioned, I wondered where the artist or artists lived. Perhaps Usher was there now, in some even more glamorous part of the world, walking through galleries and playing with new boys, better boys than me, ones that didn't challenge him in his methods or beg for his touch.

His texts had been about the service he intended me to provide, yet I was thankful that he was still communicating with me. When he had left the room the evening before with his parting words, a familiar anxiety allowed me to worry I had deviated too far from his expectations. Even with Usher nowhere near the manor and constantly reassuring myself that I had graduated far enough to secure my place, I knew not to ever take my new home for granted. If I broke his rules—even the ones I didn't know—perhaps I wouldn't be thrown back to the streets, but there was a real chance something even worse could serve as my penance.

Setting the tray in front of Darius's door, I thought about Roderick again. I wondered if he'd often been the one to deliver my meals directly. Maybe he'd contemplated doing our secret knock to let me know he was here earlier than when he'd finally let it slip on the other side of the wardrobe. Like I was now, he'd probably experienced direction from Usher telling him with some ambiguity what was expected of him.

I knew I was tasked with making Darius comfortable, but Usher also indicated that I should not reveal myself and keep out of sight if the new boy did decide to wander the house or exit his confinement. So much of me wanted to see and hug my friend, hold him and tell him he was safe—at least relatively—but I also wanted to do as I was told.

Knocking with a swift knuckle, I moved quickly around a corner to assure I would not be spotted. It wasn't as easy as I had assumed it would be to avoid Darius's gaze from his open door, and I smiled thinking about Roderick hiding from me near the exterior of my own quarters. Maybe then he'd been close enough to see me pick up the food and slide the tray into my room while I looked up and down the corridor, the way Darius was doing now, searching for the source of the materialized meal.

It felt like a trick, but a fun one, as if I'd become part of the whole mischievous plan of bringing mysterious delight to a new boy. I could see Darius studying both directions of the carpeted hallway then glancing back at the setup I'd presented on the silver tray.

"What in the hell..?" he said out loud as he brought the tray through the cracked door. I had to put my hand over my mouth so he wouldn't hear me snicker at his confusion. It was honestly pretty exciting to be on this side of the illusion, to be backstage for some portion of the grand production that was Usher's custom and see how it all came together.

When his door was closed again, I retreated back to the bookcase to fix the disaster I'd left behind in the kitchen. Being so close, I was tempted to just head to my room directly and climb into a full bathtub, clean the dried cum and food residue from my body, but Usher had instructed me to clean my own mess, and contrary to my assumption when I'd first arrived, there didn't seem to be staff in the mansion—none that I had encountered at least. It seemed, in some capacity, we were the guests as well as the help.

I removed the apron and remained naked while I scrubbed the surfaces and countertops. Uncertain if Usher was still watching, I wasn't putting on a show this time as much as I was trying to keep my clothes from getting dirty. If I was now somehow in charge of meals, there was a chance I would also have to wash my own clothing. I didn't even know where the laundry room was located, but figured if I let dirty clothes pile up, I'd eventually be getting a text with a new map to machines and cleansing powders. Hopefully in all his furnishing, Usher had provided a high-class dryer. I'd come to equate having the money to automatically dry wet clothing as truly *making it*. Peak luxury was truly rapid fabric dehydration. Admittedly, imagining a clothesline in the back courtyard strung between two of the stone men was a satisfying image in its own way.

While I laughed to myself about expensive statues supporting wet multi-colored jockstraps, a phone rang. As I searched for the source of the sound, I found one hanging on the wall not far from the monitor. It wasn't fancy like the one in my room. This was more retro than antique. While I analyzed its place in the history of communication devices, a message from Usher came in:

> *Answer the phone.*
> *Say nothing.*

How this man got anything done while observing my every move, I couldn't understand. Using the opportunity to swivel my ass toward the camera as I got to my feet, I grabbed the phone from its holder. I put the receiver to my ear, but as requested, I didn't speak.

"Um...I'm sorry, but this food is inedible, and I'm starving up here." It was Darius on the other end, insulting my cooking. "Could I get something else, please?"

I wanted to defend myself, to tell Darius that I'd never had someone in my life teach me how to cook like he had, that I'd done everything I'd seen him do; I chopped, I boiled—I even threw things into pans with oil. But I didn't respond. By Usher's orders, I could merely listen and accommodate.

Hanging up the phone, I knew the standard response was expected to be speedy. At least it had been when I'd been the one stuck in my room being served impressive treats and having my wishes fulfilled. So far, I was not providing the same level of service.

I glanced around the room and searched through the pantry until I found an unopened bag of chips, then rummaged through the fridge. Inside was a pitcher of juice. Sampling the orange liquid with a quick gulp from the side of the pitcher's rim, I tasted mangoes picked straight from the tree somehow mixed equally with oranges.

Hoping Darius would enjoy something more familiar than my terrible attempt at stew, I poured a huge glass and threw a new tray together as quickly as possible before running it up the stone passage and in front of his door. I was still unclothed when I knocked, and this time jolted all the way back to the kitchen with my sore balls bouncing lightly against my upper thighs, hoping the flourishing orchestral music in the corridor would cover my footsteps. I'd forgotten how raw my skin was from the night before until the bruises were smacking into each other. The constant sprints up and down the incline of the dimly-lit passage between the floors were already making my tender muscles ache.

Out of breath and back in front of the monitor, I discovered dials below the boxy screen. I didn't know how I'd missed them before, but I turned and pressed them until the image froze on Darius. It would have been nice to have found them earlier in the day when I'd been jerking off to empty rooms and my imagination, but technology in any form was still a blind-spot in my life.

I watched Darius drink the orange juice and eat the chips until the bag was empty, then tip it toward his mouth to consume every morsel of flavor. When he was finished, he shuffled his hands clean and piled the trash on top of the gross concoction I'd produced to put it back outside for me to retrieve. It was unclear how quickly I would need to race back up to the second floor to gather the trays, but I leaned on the counter for just a moment to collect myself. All I'd wanted after my encounter with Usher the night before was to rest. Now, I needed a bubble bath and nap more than ever. Being behind the curtain was exciting, but more than anything, it was stressful.

# Chapter Seven

Nearly done cleaning, and with the new knowledge that the monitor in the kitchen not only cycled but could be locked onto specific views, I used the textured circle to find Roderick's quarters. The screen filled with his rainbow poufs, but his bed was empty. Turning the dial again moved the view to his bathroom. I was spent for a while after the combination of my most recent interaction with Usher and pleasuring myself while cooking, but I still hoped I would catch a glance of Roderick soaping his fur in his large walk-in shower. As I used the other dial to turn the camera's angle around both rooms, I saw he was strangely absent from the opulent setting.

The phone on the nearby wall rang again. It trilled in a high-pitched and rhythmic tone a few times before I sighed and reached out to make it cease. There had been no further messages from Usher since he had instructed me to answer the first phone call, but I assumed the orders not to speak still stood as I lifted the receiver from its holder and listened.

"Alex?" the voice asked softly on the other end. It was a smart move on his part. Darius knew I didn't love being addressed by the shortened version of my name; I had corrected him and the other boys often when we'd first become acquainted. Something about the full three syllables of a name seemed more regal than my upbringing and had always made me feel important, which was amusing in a certain way, considering Usher never used any variation of my name, shortened or otherwise. I was "boy" to him or nothing. Other than the apologetic way Roderick had whispered it to me through the wardrobe, I hadn't heard my name spoken in the house at all.

It was hard to say if Darius was trying to provoke me to answer by intentionally destroying my favorite word. If I'd been permitted to talk, I would have reassured him as well as corrected him. I didn't know if I was audibly breathing the way I'd heard someone do when I'd been the one on Darius's side of the phone, when I'd held the antique cream and gold receiver in my hand asking for bubbles. At that stage, I had yet to have my first real meeting with Usher or understand how far both his generous and sadistic nature could reach in either direction.

I successfully suppressed my first instinct to respond or to let him know I was here. Rolling the cell phone Usher had given me in my other palm, I partially expected a text to come in to tell me how I should address the current situation, but nothing arrived. More than likely, Usher knew every conversation that happened in the house, even the ones on the phones that didn't seem to have a link to the outside world. If he did know what Darius was saying, that he was asking me whether I was the one fulfilling his requests, it wasn't a priority for him to give me a course of action. So I said nothing and stood quiet, just listening.

"Alright. Cool." The phone clicked when Darius hung up. He was frustrated and reasonably so. To be surrounded by so much finery after being convinced to come here by some mysterious older man, only to sit alone and hungry in a single room, he deserved more.

I stuck the phone back on the wall, feeling terrible that he was uncomfortable in the house. Not that Usher had even asked if I could cook on my houseboy application that didn't exist, but it was still my fault the level of luxury was not up to standard. Looking up to the monitor, I turned the dial back to Darius's room just in time to see him closing his bedroom door behind him.

If Darius was under the same instructions I'd received during my first day in the house, he hadn't been explicitly told to stay in his room. When I'd been the new boy, I'd chosen to stay because my bed was soft, and I had a clean bathtub around for the first time in my life. Someone had successfully managed cooking and delivering me delicious food like clockwork, so I didn't have a reason to leave. The truth was it had taken me several days to even care about what was outside of my room because I was so comfortable. But Darius wasn't, and without orders not to do so, I assumed he could explore as he pleased.

I looked down at the cell phone: no texts, no messages. Usher had told me before he left I wasn't supposed to interact with Darius or interfere with the process, but he didn't say anything about what would happen if Darius found me. Tracing the marks still present on my skin from my punishment the evening before, I thought about the whips and paddles Usher hadn't used during our session. I wondered if they were still out and waiting for me upon his return.

Even if I had accidentally violated some rule I wasn't aware existed by using the keys I'd found outside my bedroom door and using them to discover the secret passage that led to the woods, it hadn't been intentional. Perhaps that was why he hadn't restrained me while he dealt the physical punishment. The part where he forced me to watch while he jerked Darius off hadn't been expected, but the tender marks now on my thighs, ass, and chest hadn't come as a total surprise. I'd known they were due when Usher grabbed me in the woods before I could reach Darius upon his arrival. He hadn't made it a secret—before I lost consciousness—that I would pay for my transgression: leaving my room without his direct permission.

Still, being aware the beating was due hadn't made it hurt any less, and I wasn't in a hurry to give Usher new reasons to turn my ass new painful colors. Even if I wasn't going against direct orders to allow Darius to find me, I slipped the door to the passage open and slid inside to head back to my room. It simply wasn't worth the risk.

Back in my jeans and t-shirt, I left the apron on its hook and headed back through the rocky tunnel. When I reached the second floor, I surveyed the library to ensure Darius hadn't wandered inside, then slipped the bookcase closed behind me. I wondered what he would think during his solo trek through whatever Usher had left unlocked for him in the house, if he'd be impressed by the massive collection of books and art or completely freaked out by the endless unclothed otter men in compromising situations.

Violins and the reverberations of other string instruments filled the atmosphere in the empty hallway leading to my room as I poked my head around the corner to check for Darius. I tried my best to be stealthy and tiptoe across the carpet past the jewel-tone walls. There was a chance—if he was anything like I'd been when I wandered the house—he'd already headed down the spiraling stairs to find the French doors. He would discover soon enough they were locked from both sides.

I had also thought—when I'd made the journey to tug and rattle the chains on the doors myself—they were the only entrance or exit from the house. However, as I'd been led to discover, the direct path from my bedroom's wardrobe to the exterior suggested there were other hidden ways to escape. Perhaps Usher had been upset with Roderick for bringing my attention to the truth: that if I wanted to leave, I could do so at any time.

Before I collided with Usher in the woods and found myself back in my room with no idea how I'd gotten there, I explored the passage, enjoying my time in the open air on the other side, but it had never been my intention to flee. Usher must have understood that because although the ring of keys was now missing, the lock in the wardrobe had not yet been refastened. Even so, an attempted escape in any capacity wasn't a mistake I was eager to make again. The punishment was severe, and I intended to keep the information of the secret passage to myself.

Letting the door to my room creak open slowly, I planned to pop the cork on my favorite suds and strip to nothing. I wanted to soak in warm water and my new favorite scent until the bottoms of my feet and toes wrinkled. My sore body needed to roll in the large tub and dive below the surface. In my vision of the next few hours before I'd inevitably get a text from Usher telling me to make real food for dinner, I imagined blowing air from my mouth and nose while my hair and fur flowed with the waves of the cleansing water and aromas.

Instead, as I closed the door behind me and began unzipping my jeans, I heard a voice behind me. Turning quickly with my fingers still on the fly of my pants, I saw a figure sprawled across my four-poster bed. He was on his side with his hand supporting his head. "Hey girl," Darius said with a half-smile. "This is quite a room."

# Chapter Eight

"Well, I guess we're not in Beachside anymore." Darius rubbed the carved wood on one of the four posts surrounding my bed, a single finger catching in the hollow portion of a spiral and following it around the curve of the glossy dowel. I stood silent by the door, balancing the risk of punishment for making physical contact with my desperation to feel his embrace. He jumped from the bed and approached me with open arms, wide and welcoming. "Hug me, girl!"

So much of me knew I needed to pull back, that I needed to walk away or tell him to leave. Perhaps the damage hadn't yet been done, and I hadn't violated Usher's orders to avoid my friend, but I wasn't moving or speaking. Instead, when Darius was in reach, I leaped toward him, wrapping my arms around his body. I fell into his chest and let my head lean on his shoulder. My breath heaved, and within seconds, I was choking back tears. I hadn't realized how lonely I'd felt in my isolation, not until I felt the genuine warmth of Darius's body near mine.

Only a few weeks had passed since I abandoned the house we'd shared together, leaving the stained rugs and mildewed ceilings behind, but that place felt like a foggy memory now that I was among the bronze and velvet. He wouldn't understand if I had told him what I was thinking as our chests pressed together. Surrounded by golden tassels and pressed lace, textured art and smooth surfaces, I wanted to tell him the value in the bond we'd formed during our shared struggle was a currency that couldn't be spent, but it was worth more than I'd known before.

Those weren't the words that came out of my mouth, instead, I managed a few whimpers while my body convulsed to hold in the tears. He pulled back to look at me, taking in my full frame, which must have looked disheveled after being on my hands and knees for a day and a half.

"You okay?" he asked sincerely. I nodded without hesitation and wiped any water attempting escape from my eyelids.

"You?" That was honestly the more important question. I'd had time to adjust to living here, but Darius had just arrived and barely had a moment to acclimate. He walked a few steps backward to let me view his entire ensemble.

"Bitch, I am great! Look at these boots! Look at them!" He smiled and twirled in the mid-calf charcoal shoes he'd paired with pleated pastel shorts and a button-down shirt he'd tied into a crop-top to display the hair on his stomach. "Everything is designer, honey!"

"That fur though," I said pointing at the forest he'd let flourish where he used to trim or sometimes even shave.

"Well, your girl does like to please. He asked for it." I nodded in understanding. Now we both knew who "he" was: the man who had sent the camera equipment and computer to our old home, the man who owned this house.

There were so many blanks I wanted filled in about how Darius had found himself here, but when I opened my mouth to ask, he stopped me. "Listen Judy, I didn't come here to eat barbecue chips. Where's the kitchen?"

I should have taken the opportunity then to give him directions and stayed in my room. That way, I would have had some form of defense when Usher inevitably tore into my flesh with some new collection of tails. But Darius was already passed me and in the hallway, pointing his finger back and forth in either direction with a non-verbal "which way?" If the damage had already been done, I was going to enjoy some time with my friend.

Back in the kitchen yet again, Darius rounded up what was left of the stew ingredients and posed in front of the stove. He shook his hips to a beat I couldn't hear in the classical music while he cooked and talked. "There's a closet full of underwear with a guy's first and last name on the band in my room. It's incredible."

I hadn't taken Darius through the bookcase to get to the kitchen. We went the long way to the dining room where Usher had put me and Roderick on a shared leash. Luckily, I remembered the path, and every door on the way had been unlocked. Even more fortunate was my correct assumption: beyond the long table with the red runner and through the swinging door was another entrance to the kitchen.

I wasn't trying to keep information from Darius as much as trying to save him from knowing too much. Roderick's intentions had likely been pure, but the deeper he'd brought me into things without Usher's permission, the more trouble I seemed to be in. If I exposed him to more than Usher was ready for him to see, there was a chance I wouldn't be able to accept the torment for both of us. I knew as I watched Darius sway his ass in the kitchen, my intention was to do just that whenever Usher did return.

"That's what that crisp mess was supposed to be? Stew?" Darius was filling more of the air than I was with conversation, which was strange because I had so much to tell him. I worried my social skills had suffered from being secluded, but more than anything, I focused on the phone sitting in my pocket, expecting it to vibrate with a slew of messages from Usher. So far, his power seemed unlimited. If his hairy knuckles wielding a long whip somehow found their way through the touchscreen to my body, I wouldn't have been entirely surprised.

"How?" I finally asked, still tense as I watched Darius choose a knife that was probably more correct for chopping herbs and root vegetables than the one I'd selected. He didn't stop his cooking flow as he explained that he had been worried about me after we'd made contact and I'd sent him to Roderick's empty apartment. He'd spent a good chunk of time afterward asking about the previous tenant around town and giving the only name he remembered: "Roderick."

"That guy is a bad-news-gay," Darius said as he opened the top of a sealed pot and vented some of the steam inside. He pulled at his new stubbly beard as the moisture soaked into his skin. The new hair looked good on him. As attractive as Darius had always been, the hair he'd let turn to thick fuzz on his face added more allure. Considering he'd always made it a priority to shave his balls and ass, I couldn't help but wonder if the same fur had spread to even tastier areas.

"Bad news?" I asked, trying not to stare at his thighs through the leg holes of his fitted shorts.

"Yeah, girl. I get that you two were a thing or whatever, but it's good he skipped town. No one trusts—"

"Are these the same sources who told you a millionaire lived in the country with a mansion full of hairy sex slaves?" I hadn't meant to cut him off or be defensive.

For the first time, Darius turned away from his stove to look me in the eye as he motioned to everything around us. In the huge kitchen with the industrial-grade equipment and endless supply of gourmet food, his hands showcasing like Vanna White reminded me our surroundings proved at least one thing: the urban legends were true.

Turning back to the stove, Darius laughed, "And bitch said billionaire, so that better be the truth. I must have opened that webcam every night hoping you'd show up."

"What did he tell you?"

"To stop shaving."

"I thought you liked having a smooth ass," I said, laughing.

"I said I was worried about you, bitch!" Our laughter paired with the delicious smells of glutinous rice and flavored broths. "I don't hate it. Honestly, I feel sort of sexy. I see why no one else in the house bothered trimming now."

"He likes it on you," I said before thinking. If I told Darius I'd seen him with Usher, he would know I hadn't stopped it, that I'd watched the entire scene not knowing if he was enjoying himself and had even jerked off to his submission.

Darius seemed confused as he stirred what was nearing real food, and my mouth salivated for something that didn't smell like soil and rubber. After a pause and deep inhale, he kept his gaze on the food when he spoke again. "My grandmother taught me a lot of things when I lived with her. She told me there's a reason we tell each other stories that seem like they can't possibly be true." Darius plated the rice and stew as he talked, then handed me a plate with rounded edges curved like a bowl to keep everything inside. "Legends are rooted in truth and grow fastest potted with magic."

We sat on the kitchen floor with our legs zig-zagged into each other. It felt like being at home again, almost as if this could become our new sanctuary.

"I'm just glad you're safe," Darius said, patting my leg. "That's all I wanted to know for sure."

"Now I'm worried about you. You don't know what—"

Darius stopped me from talking with a sharp look then turned his sight to the camera above us. "It's okay. I know. Eat your food."

We sat with our legs pressed into each other in comfortable quiet. I wanted to tell him that as much fun as I'd had with him already, I didn't know if it was safe for us to keep seeing each other until we were given the okay. Somehow, he seemed to understand without an explanation, and as we cleaned-up and found our way back to his room, before he closed his door, he said, "Stay out of that kitchen, girl. I'm doing the cooking from now on."

# Chapter Nine

I'd gotten in the habit of locking my door since finding Darius on my bed. Portions of everything he cooked for himself showed up in front of my room, and for a while, I worried he would bump into Roderick and find out I hadn't been entirely truthful about him or our relationship. I was letting Darius assume a lot of things and keeping so much more from him.

A few days passed, and even though I kept the phone charged and near me at all times, I had only gotten silence from Usher. The lack of communication concerned me more than any threats could have. On several occasions, I considered sending him a text asking if I had done something wrong. I already knew the answer.

From under the covers, I could imagine I was anywhere and the house was anything, that the decadence belonged to me and didn't come with an unexpected exchange. In my fantasy world, I didn't live in fear of losing Usher's affection and forfeiting everything I'd gained. The weighted blankets and soft pillows were not constantly hanging like a pendulum above my head.

As soothing as the smoothness of the sheets were against me, I often found myself lying awake into the night until the sun threatened to rise outside my window. One night, a few hours before dawn would be taunting me, I heard a series of loud bangs below my room. Sitting up in bed, my body tensed, wondering if Usher was back in the mansion. I forced myself to curl back under the covers as the bangs grew louder. Soon they seemed to be outside my room and their source was now turning the knob to enter.

I put the blankets over my face and tried to be still. If it were Darius, hopefully he would remember our agreement and go back to his room. But within a few seconds, I had my answer. Keys jingled against the wood of the door until the lock turned and the door creaked open. My body wasn't ready for the punishment I knew I deserved. Usher had never come to my room before, which meant I had really fucked up by spending an afternoon with Darius. If his first priority upon return was to drag me from my bed either to be beaten or discharged, I must have really made a mistake.

He was breathing over me as I pretended to sleep. With my fists balled around the fabric of the blankets in an attempt to shield myself, I could feel my own shaking breath radiating in the enclosure I'd created. Looming closer, he shifted the bed as he leaned his weight into one of the four posts then knocked his knuckles against the wood. Three knocks. Two knocks. One knock.

I pulled the covers from my face and released myself from the humid sanctuary. Roderick stood, smiling in the darkness, bending his face into mine for a kiss.

"What are you doing!?" I whisper-yelled, rolling away from him as a reflex.

"It's okay," he said, reaching for me and stroking my hair. "I talked to Usher. He wants you to come with me." Roderick pulled at my hand.

If Usher was mad enough at me that he had contacted Roderick to relay messages, I wasn't sure if there was anything I could do to fix things. I had convinced myself I was the favorite, but it seemed if it had ever been true, it wasn't anymore.

"Hurry," Roderick said, already heading for my door.

"What do I need to wear?" I asked, jumping toward the wardrobe and ready to pick a specifically colored pair of backless underwear. If Usher was asking for me, I at least wanted to be on time. Maybe that would gain me some points to weigh against my indiscretions.

"It doesn't matter," Roderick responded. The door was open and he headed into the hallway. It had been so long since I'd seen him, and yet I couldn't fight against my own instincts to let him touch me. I threw on a pair of short trunks, then jeans and a t-shirt over them. If it didn't matter what I wore, then I would probably be picking out my last outfit. I needed to leave wearing something practical on my body for the chilly winter air and long walk back to Beachside.

Through winding hallways and stairwells I hadn't seen before, I almost felt like the house had changed itself in the night. Aside from the few paths I'd gotten used to, getting turned around in the maze of large rooms and connections was easy. Like the night I'd followed Roderick to the mansion, he led the way, seeming to have the layout memorized. He reached back for my hand as we kept a steady pace through a dark series of winding steps. I tried to resist the temptation to let our fingers connect. Roderick sensed my hesitation and looked back at me. His expression was hard to make out in the dimness, but he grabbed my hand firmly and pressed his body into mine, "It's okay, really. We have permission." Roderick put his hand on the side of my face to caress it softly then turned back, pulling me along at his speedy pace to our mystery destination.

We came to a heavy door with brass accents. Everything smelled like moist pine trees with an accent of something clean but synthetic. Roderick took the keys he'd stashed in his pocket, selected a long key similar to the one which opened the passageway in the wardrobe, and used it on the heavy lock. This was nothing like the rooms I had been disciplined in before. Beyond the chunky door were shadows and ripples of light reflected on cathedral ceilings from water. Just a few feet in front of us, beyond a paved deck surrounded by lounge chairs, was a giant indoor pool bathed in moonlight.

As I stared at the full celestial body beaming through the skylight of the massive space, Roderick began taking off his clothes next to me. Without a word, he was fully naked. Standing in the cool glow, he smiled. "Happy Birthday," he said, then got a running start and let his cannonball into the pool splash water half-way to the exposed beams of the roofing.

Roderick let his soaked hair whip around his face when he resurfaced, but I stood in shock, unsure how to respond.

"Come on," Roderick said, tapping the surface of the crystal blue water. He gave me the same big smile he always did when he was trying to convince me to do something, and before I could let anxiety take hold, I left my clothes in a heap on the deck and dove in next to him.

The water was warmer than I thought it would be, not harsh like the ocean. Being in its depth didn't feel like a battle as much as a reward. I must have been smiling when I came up for air after my dive, but didn't see him right away. Then, from behind, I felt Roderick's arms curl around my chest.

"How—" I started, grabbing his hand and leaning my nakedness into his, but he stopped me from speaking. Water dripped from my eyelashes as I his fingers traveled down my stomach.

"It's a birthday gift," he said, submerging his hand below the water's surface and between my legs. "Don't ask questions. Just enjoy it."

# Chapter Ten

Roderick caressed me in the friction of the water as I reached around to feel him growing firm against my ass. His lips found their way to my neck and offered gentle kisses while his fingertips tugged playfully at my foreskin and pulled it back to expose the head of my cock. The precum stuck to my skin just slightly despite the waves we were making, and he swirled it around my tip in a smooth motion.

I needed to face him, to feel his lips on mine again. Turning around, we pressed our torsos firmly together. Our wet fur rubbed in the comfortable warmth of the heated pool water between our bodies. I leaned my face into his, letting our short beards brush as we stood on our tip-toes, pausing at the mid-point between the shallow and deep end. With our noses side-by-side, his breath mixed with mine like we were sharing the air of everything we'd held inside since we were kids.

We could finally explore what we had always wanted with each other. Not with the lingering idea that we only stayed paired because we didn't have a choice, not because we were trying to survive, but because we wanted each other. Finally, we were living somewhere not controlled by the elements. Even if the only time we'd enjoyed each other, someone was watching and dictating our every move, controlling us in a different way, in this moment, it was just us. Me, Roderick, and this incredible sprawling space echoing our deep breathing into each other's mouths.

My hand found his neck, and I felt the space where the collar had been the night I'd finally been allowed to kiss him. The permission had come from Usher, but it had also come from myself. I'd given myself the power to love Roderick, and we were here now, somehow, alone like we'd been so many times before I'd left him. Our surroundings were the exact opposite of the thin tent and cement ground. Submerged in the immaculate pool, he brought his hand to the same spot of my neck, the area where the collars were absent. Maybe just for a night, we could pretend this world belonged to us. I let my lips find his, and we kissed hard until it felt like our interlocked bodies were gliding across the aquamarine surface.

Our momentum found us against the dark blue tile of the basin's frame where my back was against the pure-white grouted squares. I hadn't noticed before the typical music playing throughout the house was absent in the massive atrium. The only sounds in the indoor pool area were our moans and the smacking of skin. Occasionally a splash from one of our hands reaching quickly for the other would audibly reflect from the wooden plank walls, but otherwise, the stillness created an atmosphere that made me feel like the rest of the world no longer existed, and with my tongue on his, I didn't care if it did.

We shuffled together to a more shallow area, and when we arrived, I switched our positions so Roderick was against the wall. I flipped him so his elbows were resting on the deck, and my fingers found their way between his hairy cheeks and to his hole. I slipped the tip of my index finger in, and as his whine begged for me, I let my middle finger join it, stretching his tightness open and ready. Like I'd fantasized while I was in the kitchen days before, I wanted to top the boy whose smile alone made me hard. I'd waited long enough and needed to know what it felt like to be inside of him.

Roderick pushed against my two fingers until they were swallowed up to my knuckles, then further as I wiggled and parted them just slightly before pulling them out and pushing them back in. His hole was close to ready, and my cock was stiffer than I could remember it being in what seemed like years.

As I moved my fingers out and prepared my cock to replace them, unexpectedly, Roderick moved forward toward the wall. He used his hands to spin around and face me, then stuck out both legs on either side of my body, extending them before wrapping them around my back to pull me into him. My hips between his thighs, he used his hands and the buoyancy of his furry body to hover at the water's surface while holding tight to the rim.

I could see his eyes now and the way his mouth was parted with his top teeth resting on his bottom lip. His ankles locked around my back, I moved my cock back to his hole and pushed past the entrance. Roderick leaned his head back and used his legs to force the entire length of me inside of him. He moaned loudly as his tightness closed around the girth, and the shadows of the room changed in time to the growing waves.

He pushed off the wall, and I used my arms to hold him in place around me while he rode the current into a bounce, up and down from my tip to base. Leaning closer to my shoulder, the splashes and sounds of ecstasy sprang back in the nearly empty room. The unoccupied lounge chairs and stacked wooden planks, the rafters above our heads holding up the huge transparent skylight letting the full moon in—all offered us their permission to bathe in the vastness and glowing light. Roderick brought his mouth to my ear and whispered, "I've wanted this for so long," and it felt like any clouds threatening to alter the moon's luminance upon us paused in awe of our passion for each other.

Something about his words made my stomach flutter like a chrysalis exploded within me. Tiny butterflies were finally given approval to live and be beautiful. I was still incredibly hard inside him, and yet my eyes winced to hold back tears. Wetness was on my cheek, and I couldn't tell for sure if it was from the pool when I whispered back, "Me too."

We held each other for a few minutes longer until a final thrust with his arms and legs still around me sent me over the edge. I moved back to the side against the dark blue tile, all shiny and glossy near Roderick's skin, as I braced myself and prepared to shoot inside of him.

Both of our breathing was heavy, and just before I expelled my load, Roderick stopped his movement. "Wait," he said and moved so I would fall out of him. My hardness hovered in the water while I waited for him to reposition. He swam gracefully away from me and soon lay on the steps of the pool, stroking himself like a god inviting me to join his religion. I paddled over quickly and for just a moment took the opportunity of his appendage being above the water's surface to take him into my mouth. Despite the chlorine, his taste was just as I remembered, and his intoxicating scent was still present.

Now covered with a sheen of spit, I moved into position to hover over him. I was turned on enough that my hole felt ready to take him, and I swallowed every inch within me. Riding him hard, I gripped the metal loop meant to be used as a guide to lead people into the shallow end of the pool. It steadied me up and down on his cock as my arm muscles contracted with the motion, and I hoped he noticed the movement under my dark hair.

As I brought my ass flush with his pelvic bone, he grabbed at my cock and stroked it in rhythm to my momentum. In his fist, it felt like I was still fucking him, like we were somehow inside each other at the same time. Magic swirled around us. It was so overwhelming I stopped riding and had to lie next to him. I felt dizzy but reached out for his hardness. He grabbed back, and we pumped at each other with our lips and tongues connected.

"Cum with me," Roderick said, quickening his pace on my shaft. I followed his rhythm and brought my mouth back to his. As we came together, our loads spilled into the water and floated there, glistening like opals in the moonlight still shining down on us. Catching my breath with the precious stones near our skin—in the perfect nine seconds of stillness achieved by a quality orgasm—I knew if I could be anywhere in the world, it would be in this moment with him next to me forever.

# Chapter Eleven

"You didn't even realize it was your birthday, did you?" Roderick asked, leaning back on his elbows, still balanced against the steps of the giant pool. I hadn't seen them before, but below us, and extending to the deeper end, the pool floor had colored tiles creating mosaics of masculine bodies. I'd seen it done with dolphins in ritzy hotel pools, but instead of sea creatures these were supersized cocks and what resembled men playing leapfrog. I acknowledged his question with a light laugh, but still in my post-climax haze, I didn't move my focus from the newly discovered art.

He was right; I didn't exactly have a desk calendar in my room, but since it was somewhere before the end of the year and the branches were still bare outside of my window, I was probably another year older. Somehow, Roderick had remembered when I didn't. I was certain now, even if my time with him would be the only gift I received, it had still been the perfect way to celebrate.

The moon was hanging lower in the sky, and the sun didn't seem far behind. Soon the pool would change from a mystical lagoon to a warm oasis away from the chilled weather outside. I looked around at the collection of deck chairs and tables, the folded towels and sculptures; similar stone men like the ones populating the courtyard were in here, watching over what seemed to be a deserted, yet well-maintained, swimming area.

I wanted to know what it looked like during the day, if the sun rays penetrated the skylight and windows enough to let someone catch a tan, but I was still uncertain how much of the house I'd see again. If Usher allowed this gift of time with Roderick for my birthday, perhaps I was less in the red than I let myself imagine—unless it was a parting gift for the last time I would ever see either of them. But if I was no longer welcome in his home, Usher wouldn't care whether I fucked Roderick at all.

Even if I couldn't understand how it was possible, I hoped Roderick had somehow convinced him, and I wanted to know the magic words he'd used. I was finally beginning to recover from my sexual afterglow, but before I could ask Roderick for details, he was on his feet and heading up the steps. I watched the water drip from the fur on his ass as he walked to the deck and dried his body, paying particular attention to his now soft cock and any stray bits of cum still hanging in his hair. "We have another stop to make before morning comes," he said, unraveling a nearby towel for me to use.

Around me were the shiny buoyant pearls we'd left behind as I sat still partially-submerged in the comfortable temperature. I didn't question who would be tasked to fish them out and wasn't certain I cared; I only knew I didn't want the night to end. In that moment I understood for sure, I would follow Roderick anywhere.

It was a task to bring myself to my feet, but once I did, the towel was immediately around me, along with Roderick's arms. He ran the soft fibers down the arc of my chest and stomach, absorbing the dampness of my own fur. I wanted to dive back in the pool to skinny dip and play longer, or sprawl out on the slatted lounge chairs to see if we could fill our balls up enough to fuck again, maybe this time on a mostly flat surface.

Instead, Roderick was slipping his jeans over his still slightly moist body, and I followed. We left my new favorite location behind to wander through more twisting hallways in the unfamiliar parts of the labyrinth. With Roderick guiding me by the hand though it all and my boots hanging at my side, I let my bare feet leave moist prints along our path across the lush carpet.

A few things began to look familiar: a burgundy wall here, a carved bust of a man with a gag in his mouth that mimicked a funnel there. I'd never seen one in person before, but the way the gag's style parted his lips, I could only imagine what liquids he was prepared to receive down his throat. If I ever did get a chance to have a real conversation with Usher, there were endless amounts of important things I should to ask, but many of my thoughts lingered on the art, and more than anything, I wanted to know where the pieces came from and whether real men had posed for each of his selections.

From the hue of the walls, I assumed we were somewhere on the first floor, not far from the red room. Roderick still had his keys jingling from his hip but didn't use them right away when we stopped at a flat wall which appeared to be our destination. Centered on the satin surface was a new stone man balanced on a pedestal. At its base were words etched into the granite with letters I couldn't make out in the dimness.

We stood at the dead end for a moment before Roderick dropped my hand. It was the first time he'd released me since exiting the atrium. He reached out his finger to circle each erect nipple of the statue, then stood tall on the tips of his toes to whisper something into the shaped rock's ear. When he finished, he smirked in my direction, checking to see if I was at all amused by his demonstration. I was.

The stone man didn't change his expression, instead turning in a semi-circle on the base and retracting to one side with a mechanical sound. Behind where he had stood guard, there was a red door.

"Seriously?" I said, smiling.

"Seriously." Roderick reached for his keys and shoved a long one with chunky teeth toward the lock.

"This house is so fucking strange."

"Just wait," he said, pushing the heavy door open. On the other side was only darkness until Roderick ran his hand along the interior wall and located a switch. With a click, the area was slightly illuminated, and before me was a series of buttons, monitors, and microphones. The endless array of knobs and dials added up into a collection of boards and panels with various green, yellow, and red lights flashing out of sync with each other.

Beyond the boards, at eye-level, was a mirror. I could see Roderick and myself reflected in it, partially clothed with wet hair. But when Roderick pushed a button on the panel, a light came on beyond the mirror to reveal a large space with dark walls, metal surfaces and black blocks, big toys and whips, and a huge cross with restraints. The red room. From this spot, I could see everything that happened inside.

# Chapter Twelve

Right now, the room through the mirror sat empty. Standing there, I felt moved for the first time to call it a dungeon. All the elements inside formed bars and cages composed from walls of sex objects, rods, and shining chains. It hadn't been as noticeable when I was inside of it all.

Taking in the sight, I wondered how many times someone had been in the control room while I was being beaten or fucked, if they'd observed my vulnerability from the safety of this side of the mirror. The one I hadn't taken much notice of when I was sitting confused with cum dripping out of my hole, silently waiting on multiple occasions for a man who never returned.

Roderick moved from the controls toward a desk against the wall behind us. It looked out of place with the high-tech equipment around, almost ancient, and was equipped with a rolling lid that locked at the bottom. If I were one of those men, the gays who wear loafers and roll their vintage pants to their ankle to shop for high-end antiques, I probably would have appreciated its design more. For me, possessing second-hand items was more of a consequence of my tax bracket than a method of demonstrating my taste level. Knowing I could pull the same clothes and furniture from any dumpster; to me, *antique* and *vintage* just seemed to be the acceptable words assigned to owning something out of fashion for an astronomical price.

With his endless set of old and new-looking keys, Roderick bent down and took a smaller one to the bronze lock. As he lowered himself, I could see the hair between his ass peeking out from the top of his jeans when they scooted down his hips. We'd walked long enough from the pool to the new location that I was ready to go again, and the sight of the dungeon's various structures and hanging tools registered like muscle memory to a very particular muscle. I hadn't bothered trying to slide underwear onto my wetness and could feel my hardness pushing against the chill of the jean's zipper. I wanted to top Roderick again, bend him over the rolling desk, to see if his hole would open as quickly for me as it had the first time.

Walking closer, I hovered above him, hoping he would notice my firmness through the denim near his face and pull me from my pants, that he would stay on his knees near the desk to put me in his mouth for just a minute. Morning felt near, and I wanted to spend whatever time we had left with the moon close to Roderick's body. Even in this new room with my new view, all I could think about was fucking until the sun came up and making us both spend another load.

Roderick continued pressing the small key into the tight hole until something finally clicked, and he pushed up on the roll top desk. He hadn't noticed while kneeling that I was trying to make a move on him. Once he rose to his feet and the lid chugged in a rolling pattern until it stopped, he looked down at the bulge in my pants and smiled. He reached out to give my boner a playful squeeze, then immediately turned back to the open desk.

"You need to see this," Roderick said, finally looking at me. Inside the desk were papers and small boxes, books and envelopes. He bypassed touching the peak in my jeans again while he reached out for a file. "You should know," he said, putting the collection of papers in my hands. I was disappointed but tried to bring my attention to the text and ignore the way his lips glistened. It took all my focus to let my fingers trace over the dark ink instead of putting them through his hair so I could direct his mouth to the pulsing under my pants.

On the front cover, outlined in an embossed gold frame, were words I didn't understand:

> *Son coeur est un luth suspendu;*
> *Sitot qu'on le touche il resonne.*

They looked liked the collection of letters on the statue outside the entrance, but I couldn't tell if they were the same. When I opened to the pages, pictures were pasted inside and held down with tape on all four corners. They were pictures of young men I'd never met before surrounded by details outlining specifics about their bodies: their height, weight, current location. Each profile contained a section regarding body hair that was highlighted and circled several times over.

I looked up at Roderick, unsure what I was supposed to be seeing in the file. It didn't mean anything to me. He reached out to flip forward a few pages until a familiar face was staring back at me.

Roderick moved away when I reached his image and sat in a wheeled office chair at the controls. I could hear him spinning in circles as I continued to read the stats under his profile. If the date was correct, he had been in the house with Usher since just after the night I'd left him in the tent. It was my fault; I had driven him here to this lifestyle. Maybe Usher had selected him, but I'd put him in the position to figure out what to do without me.

"Keep going," he said, seeing that I was lingering on his paperwork. I flipped the page to see an even more recognizable face: mine. My stats and description paired with a picture of me laying on my side in white briefs in my old bed.

Surprisingly, I looked impressive on paper. My cock size—in centimeters instead of inches for some reason—stood out, and next to my name was a gold star with the inked word:

*Postulant.*

The next page was another face I knew, Darius, but he didn't have the same phrase or colors near his name. There were more pages after him, but I turned back to Roderick's profile first. I wasn't the only one. Next to his pictures, he had an accolade in the same position.

*Novitiate.*

I faced Roderick while I read the word out loud like a question. He sighed and bit his lip, then looked at the ceiling and spun a few more times in the cushioned chair behind the control board. He seemed to be contemplating if he had already gone too far, if he had let me see too much. Sensing his hesitance, it all hit me at once.

"I'm not supposed to be in here, am I?" Roderick stopped circling but didn't face me. He tapped his fingers nervously near the flashing lights and buttons with reluctance. "Tonight—all of it—did we have permission?" My voice grew louder as he looked up to stare through the clear window into the red room and all its fixtures, still avoiding my eyes.

"I spend a lot of time here, alone," he said, fingering one of the knobs to let the light in the dungeon dim and glow fluorescent over and over again.

"Did we have permission?" I needed an answer.

"You had to know," he said, shaking his head as he turned the dial all the way down and let the room beyond the transparent mirror darken. I threw the collection of papers back to the desk.

"Why?" My voice was even louder, and I felt angry tears welling up inside. Every beautiful butterfly became a knot in my stomach, knowing he had deceived me—again.

Roderick lowered his gaze once more and ran his flattened hands over all the buttons of the control board to create a quiet clicking sound. When he stopped at a small lever, he pushed it to the middle position until the room we stood in was showered with moderate white light.

The new level of brightness revealed things in the control room I hadn't been able to see before. It was bigger than I had originally thought and extended out in one direction not far from the roll top desk toward a velvet curtain. The burgundy panels were accented beneath a single spotlight and reminded me of a secret back room in a gay book shop.

Roderick nodded toward the closed curtain, rose to walk over, and parted the hanging fuzzy lips for me to enter. I couldn't see anything beyond them but needed answers, so I ducked my head through the opening and let my body follow. Behind me, Roderick closed the drapes and stood inside of them while he flipped another switch.

Tiny spotlights on the wall lit up, each illuminating a different portrait hanging in place. They were evenly spaced out and similar in artistry, but as Roderick watched me take them all in, I could see the obvious differences between them.

Some were painted and some were photographs, but none of the images were dated. In sets of two, the first portrait was always a standing man in a suit with a boy on his knees next to him like an obedient pet wearing a collar. But they weren't the fabric or neoprene collars with fun colors. The chokers in the pictures were solid and silver with massive locks mounted like a charm holding the ring together. I couldn't read the tiny text, but each collar had engraving which seemed to match the language I'd seen on the front cover of the file and the statue which had been guarding the room.

I wanted to ask Roderick if he knew what the words meant, but the anger was still red hot inside of me. If I turned toward him now and saw his face, I wasn't certain if I would cry or lunge at him. Even as I continued to explore the portraits, I wondered if the intimacy we shared in the pool had been real at all. If it had all been part of a scheme, I didn't want to know. Not right now.

There was empty space beyond the last hanging portrait, but it was the final entry which stopped me where I stood. Younger and naked, on his knees next to a fully-clothed man, was... Usher. However, on the plaque below, the name "Usher" was not accompanying his likeness. None of the pictures mentioned the name of kneeling boys at all. In fact, like every picture before it, the title of "Usher" was always under the standing man.

I gasped at the sight and covered my mouth. Jumping back, I prepared to finally face Roderick and ask what it all meant. I had to know why he brought me here, why he had let us fuck without permission and created such an elaborate evening to lead me to this place. I needed to know what he wanted me to do now. But as I turned to him, I was directly grabbed by the neck and hair. Roderick was gone, and in his place was Usher forcing me to the ground under his strong hands.

"This was not meant for your eyes, boy." He had returned to the house. Surrounded by the museum of centuries of chosen boys, I fell on my knees to the carpet below at his mercy. My knees rubbed into the woven fibers under his force while his glare penetrated every orifice of my body. He grabbed around the roots of my hair to tighten his hold. Despite the pain, I couldn't help noticing that he looked older somehow. His facial hair looked even more grey than it had when he had first begun letting the salt portion fill around the darker spots.

As confused and terrified as I was, he looked incredibly sexy, and if he had fucked me right then and there—forced his cock into my mouth or let knees scrape and burn on the thick carpet as he moved me around his dick—I would have been grateful. But similar to the day in the woods when he found me with the shells and phone by the tree, like he seemed to be able to do any time he made a boy cum, everything went black.

# Chapter Thirteen

The best night I had ever had in the house had quickly become the worst night. Suns and moons rose and set while the occasional frost collected outside the single window in my room on the branches below. My room had again become a prison.

Usher must have accepted Darius as the new head chef in the house or had again tasked Roderick with the responsibility. I was receiving meals, nothing special, but food. My basic necessities, aside from attention, were being met. Unfortunately, the purple bathtub and giant bed had lost their appeal as I paced the same square footage over and over throughout the course of each day. The phone I had been gifted had gone missing from the room. Like Usher's communication with me, it too seemed to have been revoked.

Every source of pleasure felt tainted now. Even jerking off when my cock got hard thinking about fucking Roderick in the pool was overshadowed by his betrayal. Fantasizing about Usher was clouded by my own itemized lapses in judgement. Not only had I interacted with Darius; I'd cum before Usher's return. Even worse, it had been at the hand of someone he had told me specifically not to be intimate with outside of his presence. I wasn't sure how heavily seeing the control and portrait rooms would be weighed after all of that, but I knew my indiscretions had led me to a punishment worse than physical pain. Solitary confinement.

A quick knock on the door stopped me from pacing valleys into the rug. I didn't rush for my food, but when I brought the tray in and began unpacking my lunch, a folded piece of paper fell out. I doubted it was from Usher but the handwriting and message confirmed it:

*Get me out of here girl.*

Darius. Something had happened to him while I'd been locked away. I hadn't been able to watch out for him while trapped behind my door, and now, for whatever reason, he wanted to leave.

Along with the note was a pen which I took as an indication he expected an immediate reply. I walked toward the wardrobe and, pushing the clothes aside, surveyed the back panel. Either Usher didn't know the lock still hadn't been resealed, or he didn't care. He probably kept the passage open as a challenge to me, to see what I would endure before considering an escape back to a more simple place. As if I could retreat to a time before I knew about tea cakes, infused bath products, and strange competitions within a seemingly enchanted spooky sex house.

Grabbing the pen, I scrawled a quick message on the blank side of the note and slid it under the door. I couldn't see his hands or fingers, but the paper disappeared into the hallway as something pulled the words I'd chosen:

*Be ready to leave tonight.*

I wasn't certain if any of it was "designer" like Darius had commented on his own curated clothing, but I'd developed a sort of "go-bag" now with my favorite outfits and boots. After the countless times I'd let myself believe I was about to be extracted from the house, I'd packed them along with a few extra pairs of skimpy underwear. I wrapped what remained in the glass bottle of lavender bubbles safely in some slutty knee-high socks then stashed it in a section of a gym bag I'd found in the jockstrap drawer.

Waiting until the moon seemed high enough, I pushed the latch on the back panel of the wardrobe open. Surveying the state of my room one last time—the four-poster bed, throw pillows, and giant television that would never be in my budget—I closed the panel behind me.

Using my hands to guide me along the rocky surfaces and around a corner, as I'd suspected, the tunnel did connect to other areas. There was a chance every secret passage joined at some point to match the intricate maze inside the house. But tonight, I had only one destination in my mind and just hoped I was going the right direction.

My fingers answered my questions in the darkness until they found slight creases in the stone that gave way to a more wooden texture. Pressing my body against it, I listened with my ear flush to the new panel. With no voices, I whispered my call into the flatness, "Darius?"

His answer was immediate. "Omg girl, where even are you?" He had to have been listening all night, waiting for me to find him. I tried to explain where I was in the passage without speaking too loudly, but more importantly, I needed to know if there was a lock on his end.

"Well shit," he said in response to my inquiry. I was about to turn around to come up with a new plan but heard, "One sec" as his footsteps traveled away from earshot. A few minutes later, I heard light pecking against the wood before the panel opened and Darius stood framed by his expensive clothing hanging on either side. He held up a thin sounding rod with a pointed end and smiled. "Skills," he said, letting the slim rod fall to the rocky ground with a high-pitch ting.

"Skills," I agreed, feeling his arms around me in a tight but quick embrace. As much as I had learned living on my own, Darius was endlessly resourceful. His family hadn't abandoned him the way mine had, but when they were no longer around and he made his move to Beachside, he'd taught himself more than I could ever imagine learning in order to survive.

"I swiped that after that first time he used it," Darius said as I led him through the passage and back toward the area I knew would lead to the woods. "Call me vanilla. I mean, I can do some pain, but your girl needs some pleasure with her Rocky Road." I'd never seen the sounding rods among Usher's collection of toys myself and wondered if it was something specific he had chosen for Darius. "You liked him though, didn't you?"

"Roderick?" My stupid brain was letting my mouth move on its own again.

"Wow. What? No. I mean, you liked what *he* did to you?"

I wasn't sure how to answer, how to tell Darius that it wasn't the same for me with Usher as it seemed to be for the other boys. "I can only take so much bruising on this body without some dick to make it better," Darius said, lifting his shirt to reveal slash-like marks on his chest. I nodded in acknowledgement, pointing toward my own sore places.

"You don't have to tell me why," I said as we got closer to what I hoped was the end of the passage. It was more difficult to navigate without the sun providing a sliver of light to guide us.

"It's Sonny mostly," Darius said as I pushed at the wall for the hidden door. He admitted that after weeks in the house, away from home, he wasn't sure his favorite half-boy, half-house-cat, was feeding himself. Like me, he hadn't known before coming to this mansion the expectation was for him to permanently relocate.

With the stone door pushed aside, I looked out to the stillness of the woods and I dangled my foot over the threshold to find the dirt below. Grabbing Darius's hand and helping him out of the house, I watched as he walked into the dense trunks.

I didn't follow.

"Come on, girl!" he said, walking back in my direction and holding out his hand for mine. "It's not worth it. All the pain to be stuck in a fancy room all day and just taken out to be used?"

I laughed a little and shrugged, "It's the same gig. The clothes are just fancier." Darius pulled his hand back and stood in the clearing with the hair below his crop top blowing in the breeze. Only the wind whistled through the remaining leaves in the silence between us as I brought my view to the frozen ground.

"I'm staying," he said, breaking the strange quiet to bring his foot back over the threshold.

I blocked his way inside. "I can't protect you here, and you can't protect me either." Half in and half out, he knew what I said was true. "Please go, for Sonny. For Brent and Marco even."

I must have rolled my eyes when I mentioned the bleach-blonde brothers who came to Beachside for the surfing and cock because Darius laughed. Even as roommates, they had never been my favorite people. I didn't go out of my way to talk to them much, but I understood enough to know they were probably totally lost at home without Darius.

"If they haven't burned that place down yet, it will be a surprise for all of us," Darius said, nodding. I'd never thought much about how Darius took care of not only me, but all the boys. It didn't seem to be a position he had sought but just organically accepted. Unlike me, he just couldn't see a boy struggle if he knew he could help.

"I'm sorry you ever came here and—"

Darius cut me off abruptly but was calm as he spoke. "You know I had to...but I also wanted to."

A fresh silence hung between us as we looked into each other's eyes. I shifted my focus to his lips before I spoke. "Just get home safe," I said, leaning my body closer to his and letting our mouths align.

He held me close, and we swayed together as we straddled the passage's exit. With nothing else to say, he brought his lips to mine. We'd kissed before on the night we messed around and shared little pecks since then, to say hello, to say goodbye, to say thank you…for everything. But this time, our lips lingered longer than usual, and for just a moment, our tongues sparked in a way that felt electric. It was friend-tongue for a strange experience we'd shared together, non-verbal appreciation for us both risking our lives in order to save each other.

With his taste still on me, when our lips separated, he said, "What will he do to you when he finds out?"

I didn't know the answer, but I handed him the go-bag. When he took it, I said, "Have the boys clean the tub at home. I think Sonny will fit in the boots."

Darius sighed and turned toward the dark woods. I didn't have a flashlight to give him, but I hoped the sun would be up soon enough to guide his path. "I better not find out you're still messing with that Roderick guy."

I nodded instead of taking the chance of telling him the truth about Roderick living in the house, the truth about anything. It was safer for him if he didn't know.

"I can't believe I grew a damn beard out to be here. What a waste."

"Don't shave. It looks sexy on you," I said with a wink that for some reason made my throat tighten like tears were not far behind. Luckily, Darius shook his head and disappeared into the depths of the foliage before a single warm droplet found the top of my cheek.

# Chapter Fourteen

When breakfast didn't arrive the next morning, I knew it would only be a matter of time before Usher discovered Darius was missing. Whether learning that would force Usher's hand to acknowledge I was still up here, I could only hope. Even if he burst through my bedroom door and dragged me by the scruff to be tied spread eagle and feel his boot on my cock, or ripped off all my clothes and used every stinging whip on my body, or shoved the biggest plug he possessed inside my hole without a warm-up—I could deal with any level of pain if he would just feed me his attention.

By lunch, I was offered minimal sustenance, but more importantly, another note was paired with my food. It wasn't friendly like the one I'd received from Darius. If the handwritten words were any indication, not only had it been discovered that Usher's newly appointed head chef was missing from his manor, but he knew I'd been the one to help him escape. Adding that fact on top of everything I'd already done to offend the master of the castle, I knew even more severe punishment was in my immediate future.

In the swirls and dips of Usher's impressive handwriting, the note commanded:

> *Downstairs,*
> *now.*

No specifications were outlined as far as the proper attire. Despite winter being fully upon us, no seasonal underwear had been requested. At this point, I would have liked to have been asked to wear a festive jockstrap, something red with candy canes or tinsel-decorated pine trees, or maybe a set of reindeer horns to go with a bright green pair of tight briefs so he could order me to prance around before he turned my ass cheeks the color of poinsettias in full-bloom.

When I arrived on the first floor, the passage beyond the credenza was already open, its mysteries revealed and lighting a clinical white instead of the dim scarlet wash I'd come to associate with the scenery from my previous experiences. Not unlike the last time Usher had left me alone inside, the full-power overhead lights felt like seeing a peeled watermelon. Whole, raw, and exposed. No modesty or caution. The room at the end of the hall highlighted all the equipment and toys, along with what must have been weeks' worth of bodily fluids. My own dried cum, near the block I'd sat on to watch Usher's first encounter with Darius, chipped when I walked my bare feet across it.

The huge rectangle of the two-way mirror reflected my frame. Beside me, in the reproduced image, I noticed something new in the room. Piled together was a bucket, a mop, and a collection of cleaning supplies. While I poked at a lemon-yellow set of rubber gloves hanging over the bucket, I wondered if I would be serving Usher his custodial fantasy until I spotted an inked piece of paper. Near the unsexy hand accessories of my new janitor costume, another note simply read:

*Clean up, boy.*

Maybe he didn't have a fetish for sanitation, but by the time I was on my hands and knees taking a soapy sponge to the cement floors, I knew he was right about it needing to be done. The way the spots of lubricant and cum were layered upon each other on every surface made it difficult to determine what the original liquid had been. Whether each overlapping splatter was synthetic or natural bodily fluids, the space was in desperate need of purification.

Not far from the table and walls full of sex toys were special supplies for cleaning the variety of dildos and plugs. Some were so big I wondered who was actually able to fit them in their body. Holding each of them between my hands made them feel giant and bulbous. If they had been seeds, they would have grown into redwoods.

An interesting thing about gay men is the way masculinity manifests itself within us. Being the biggest and strongest isn't an instinct that disappears; it just becomes something more exciting. Instead of lifting heavy objects, we see if we can impress a sexual partner by showing them how much we can fit in our holes. Puffing out our rainbow crests and chests, taking pain for each other and calling it pleasure, we prove our manhood through servility. The practice lies on some pastel-colored Venn diagram where submission and power overlap. People who enjoy taking toys and dick want the challenge as much as the glory. It's virtually unspoken and would change everything if we ever did admit it, but truly, bottoms, regardless of gender, are the most powerful people in the world.

There were more toys mounted to the wall, silicone dicks and polyurethane tubes that looked like snakes meant to wind long and deep into a boy's ass. An industrial size bottle of lube, matching the one I'd seen in Roderick's fake apartment, sat in the corner drizzling slowly onto the same spot like a drip castle, the kind I'd made with wet sand as a kid on the beach where the moist sand would build onto the dryer portions until it became a solid tower. Searching for something among the supplies I'd been given, I didn't find anything designed to destroy a fortified castle made from artificial precum.

It took hours to glide each smooth toy through my hands and polish it until the different colored plastics and silicones were shining and returned to in their assigned spots. I wiped down each bench and restraint. Everything smelled like citrus from using the foaming dust spray to make the wood of the Saint Andrew's Cross sparkle under the bright lights. Even if I wouldn't be using the space any time soon, it was nice to have it smelling less like a neglected locker room for once. I knew the scent of man and sexual pheromones would return soon enough and hopefully I would be part of producing them again.

Other than punishing me with manual labor, Usher's reason for deciding that now was the time to clean everything was confusing, but more than anything, I was just glad to be finished. With the supplies packed away I headed toward the door. The lights turned off as I opened it. Looking back to the two-way mirror and control room, I smiled through the darkness, hoping whoever had turned the dial to zero had enjoyed watching me scrub and stroke each toy.

The various chemicals I was covered in penetrated my nose as I exited the hallway, and I didn't bother trying to close the credenza panel behind me. A breeze pushed the hair on my forehead and felt refreshing after inhaling overpowering pine and orange for what must have been several hours. It was coming from in front of me, and to my surprise, the French doors—the ones that always seemed bolted shut—were wide open. The thin white curtains were blowing in a crisp breeze from a winter temperature that always threatened to become frost, but rarely did.

Leaning against the tall doors were garden shears and tools with long wooden handles. *No.* I approached with caution and pulled at a piece of paper taped to the glass and flapping in the wind:

*You're not done yet, boy.*

Seeing the doors open for the first time since I'd arrived made me think about what it would be like to run through them, to leave with just what I had on my body and turn the corner through the courtyard and into the woods. I could follow the half-loop back to the end of the brick and past the gates that were rusted and welded shut, cross the train tracks and return to a still complicated and yet simplified life. But I'd proven something to myself the night before as I'd stood at the threshold kissing Darius goodbye—despite the punishment growing like a hunger within me, I craved Usher's attention for a reason. There was little he could do to drive me away. This was my home, it was my life, and I wanted to stay.

If learning how to landscape would get me any closer to atonement, I was willing to dig in the dirt for a while. Luckily, my new sexy gear included a set of gardening gloves. As cold as it was, I decided to take my chances and remove everything I was wearing. My shirt and pants were all moistened with fluids anyway. I disrobed until I was in nothing but a jockstrap and the gloves, then I slung the gardening hoe over my shoulder. If he wouldn't give me his attention, I would take it.

I'd never had the chance to admire the flowers in the light of day. Their colors were much more vibrant, and as I knelt near a nearly overgrown bed, their scent was just as impressive. I dug my fingers into the soil while I looked up at a chiseled man plotted at the center of the garden. His shadow cast over me made me feel small, and at the base, carved into the rock, was again the phrase I didn't understand:

*Son coeur est un luth suspendu;*
*Sitot qu'on le touche il resonne.*

It could have been the nearly frozen earth up to my elbows or exhaustion from sweeping clean an entire fall season's worth of leaves from the spiral stones leading to the house, but as I looked up to the man, soaking in his defined jaw under the caved scruff, the tight band around his waist cupping his round ass—I heard the translation clearly:

*"His heart is a tightened lute;*
*as soon as one touches it, it echoes."*

# Chapter Fifteen

With the courtyard cleared and the dungeon pristine, I was still uncertain what Usher had been preparing for with the sudden sterilization of the manor. Finally submerged in my beloved tub and fighting off intrusive thoughts about further labor, I knew hours had passed since I'd eaten anything. As the evening edged to what felt like close to midnight, my stomach ached with hunger. I'd spent so much energy cleansing the spaces and could only assume the physical and mental torment would continue into the next day. I wanted to be prepared and continue serving my sentence, but it seemed dinner would not arrive on its own. Not only was I being starved of human interaction, but now even the privilege of my meals had been revoked.

My bedroom door was unlocked, which I took as an invitation to feed myself. Slipping on a pair of white briefs, I left my shoes behind knowing they really didn't go with the outfit. The stone of the passage in the shortcut between the second-floor library and kitchen was cold against my feet, but I wanted to be prepared in case I did run into Usher. More likely, he would continue to avoid me in the expansive house. But on the off-chance I did encounter him, I wanted to look sexy—not in a way that made it look like I was trying to get his attention but more so as if it had been a total accident that I happened to be wearing a similar ensemble to the one I'd had on the first time I jerked off for him when I knew he was watching.

Munching on some chips while leaning against the counter, I looked up into the camera fixed to the corner of the kitchen. The day my roommates had helped me set up all the equipment Usher had sent to our house, the computers, cameras, and various cables I didn't understand, his voice had gotten me hard even before I had seen his face. Perhaps it was knowing how much money a man had been willing to spend to buy my time, that he thought I was worth not only the effort, but that I deserved more than I had been born into. Lying there on my old sheets with my dick popping from my waistband, I'd felt like royalty.

The memory alone was making me firm below the thin white cotton, and I didn't break my stare with the lens of the mounted camera as I put my chips on the counter and let my hand drift down my torso. My hair felt soft as I brought a finger under the elastic and let it flick at the head of my cock. I could already feel the precum leaking out as I circled it around and hoped Usher was watching. He had power over me because I desired the home he'd made for me as much as I wanted his touch. But I'd forgotten my own power, that as much as I craved him, he craved me even more. I would regain not only his attention but his full affection.

A few minutes passed as I brought my other hand to my chest and pinched at my own nipples beneath the hair. They stiffened quickly, and I circled them with spit from my tongue while I teased the release of my cock through the top of the briefs. It all felt so familiar, like the day I'd first felt Usher's presence in the woods and imagined him tasting the sweat on my stomach, like the moment he commanded me to cum and the words rang through my mind until I shot on the forest floor.

The memory made my balls feel full, and as I brought the elastic down below them to push my cock up higher and on display, I let myself believe it would only be a matter of minutes before Usher burst through the door to forgive me for everything I'd done. In no time, I'd be bent over the counter with his cock inside me, pumping together until we both came.

I wanted to wait to cum, to keep myself hard for as long as possible and give him time to find his way to me. But my imagination was spiraling with vivid images of Usher and our mutual need to please each other. Whether I wanted to or not, I was about to burst. Squeezing lightly at my own balls and stroking faster, I prepared to shoot, but a loud bang stopped me where I stood. Dropping my grip on my cock, the sounds of metal on metal grew louder. My arousal turned quickly to fear, but the excitement remained.

With my hardness still sticking out above my tight underwear and exposing the top of my ass, I turned around to flip the monitor on. I wanted to know the source of the noise, but as I cycled through the empty rooms, I saw nothing. As if black material had been put over every other camera, each shot was dark. Messing with the dials in an attempt to fix the lack of color, I moved something that suddenly made the sound come through speakers I hadn't realized existed below the glass screen. All this time there had been audio, it was just turned down. I wish I had known earlier, when I'd been using it as my own personal jerkoff material.

Continuing my channel surfing, I changed the buttons until the sound of the bangs were the loudest. The screens were still black, but in one corner of the loudest broadcast was a static face that seemed very familiar. He wasn't human, but I knew where to find him.

Putting my cock away, I was still pulsing with warmth but growing soft. I left the kitchen through the dining room and followed the path I'd only taken on my knees before, when Roderick and I had been attached by our collars and led by Usher. That night, I'd found myself kneeling and taking his spit inside me. Coincidentally, the same eerie tones seemed to be playing as they had that night during the ritual.

It was a guess, but I bypassed the entrance to the grand foyer where I would have run into the French doors and credenza, instead following the back end of a path that had been revealed to me only days before. There, protecting the doorway, was the stone man I'd seen on the monitor, the one Roderick had introduced me to. His eyes seemed more welcoming somehow, more familiar, as if the statue recognized me and beckoned me to enter. The translation his friend had whispered to me in the courtyard echoed in my mind, and I hovered on the tips of my toes to reach his large ear. I vocalized the words in English, hoping he would understand, and felt the hair on my face tickling my lips against the stone as I spoke.

The carved man seemed to smirk in a half-smile before moving aside and revealing the door. I didn't have a key like Roderick's, but it didn't matter because the door was open as if someone had been inside recently. Beyond it, the colored lights cascaded on the control board. Through the two-way mirror, in the red glow of the freshly cleaned dungeon, Usher stood tall in his suit. Next to him, naked and holding a silver tray from the kitchen, was Roderick.

Inching closer to the glass, I could see that although Roderick's bottom half was out and exposed, he had something metal covering his cock. The enclosure looked tight around him, like a cage looping around his balls and preventing him from getting erect. His collar was in place but in addition was a matching ball-gag buckled tightly around his cheeks and fastened in the back.

I leaned over the controls and flashing lights for a better look. In the area that had been out of my vision when I entered, closer to the floor of the dungeon, were more familiar faces, large bare feet, and furry asses framed in backless underwear. Each lined-up round backside was resting on heels, toes curled to keep each boy in position with their knees spread apart and hairy chest leaning forward.

On the tray Roderick held was a modest collection of whips. As Usher grabbed a familiar one with a single tail from the shining surface, he waved it in front of the formation. In view of their worried eyes, he paused with the whip in his hand and looked up to the two-way mirror. I didn't think he could see me, but I stood frozen anyway, as if he were a deadly predator whose vision was based solely on movement. I could hear my own shallow breathing out of time with the moans and whimpers coming from the kneeling boys as I waited for him to make his next move.

Finally, Usher smiled, ran his hand through one of the captive's long mane of hair, and winked devilishly in my direction. Returning to his kneeling line of boys, he moved his lips around to prepare a generous amount of spit. All on their knees in the scarlet hue with collars around their necks and mouths wide open below Usher were Brent, Marco, Sonny...and Darius.

The End

# Leo Sparx

Leo Sparx is a digital artist who is bringing his fascination with the history of queer sex to the literary erotica world. Inspiration for his work is often found during virtual orgies, trips to offbeat museums, or classic—occasionally spooky—literature. His unique blend of steamy sensations and dark passion takes the reader on a kinky exploration and allows them to experience encounters in unexpected locations.

www.leosparx.com

instagram.com/authorleosparx

twitter.com/authorleosparx

authorleosparx@gmail.com

## More Leo Sparx Books

Claiming Alexander
Taming Alexander
Saving Alexander

## 4 Horsemen Publications

## LGBT

### Grayson Ace
### (erotica)

How I Got Here
First Year Out of th Closet
You're Only a Top?
You're Only a Bottom?
I Think I'm a Serial Swiper

### V.C.Willis
### (Fantasy Romance)

The Prince's Priest
The Priest's Assassin
The Assassin's Saint
The Saint's Bloodeater

## Erotica

### Honey Cummings

Sleeping with Sasquatch
Cuddling with Chupacabra
Naked with New Jersey Devil
Laying with the Lady in Blue
Wanton Woman in White
Beating it with Bloody Mary
Beau and Professor Bestialora
The Goat's Gruff
Goldie and Her Three Beards
Pied Piper's Pipe

### Dalia Lance

My Home on Whore Island
Slumming It on Slut Street
Training of the Tramp
72% Match
It was Meant to Be... or Whatever

### Ali Whippe

Office Hours
Tutoring Center
Athletics
Extra Credit
Bound for Release
Fetish Circuit

www.ingramcontent.com/pod-product-compliance
Lightning Source LLC
Chambersburg PA
CBHW050156110726
47898CB00008B/2828

* 9 7 8 1 6 4 4 5 0 1 4 0 5 *